John William Kirton

Dr. Guthrie

Father Mathew. Elihu Burritt. Joseph Livesey

John William Kirton

Dr. Guthrie
Father Mathew. Elihu Burritt. Joseph Livesey

ISBN/EAN: 9783337423681

Printed in Europe, USA, Canada, Australia, Japan

Cover: Foto ©Andreas Hilbeck / pixelio.de

More available books at **www.hansebooks.com**

Dr. Guthrie.

Father Mathew. Elihu Burritt.

Joseph Livesey.

BY

JOHN WILLIAM KIRTON, LL.D.,

Author of " Buy your own Cherries," " Happy Homes, and How to Make them," &c. &c.

CASSELL & COMPANY, Limited:

LONDON, PARIS, NEW YORK & MELBOURNE.

1885.

CONTENTS.

DR. GUTHRIE,

SCOTLAND'S TEMPERANCE WORTHY.

———◦⋄◦———

IT is a remarkable fact that the two things with which Dr. Guthrie's name is most widely known, Temperance and Ragged Schools, should both have had their origin in what appears at first sight to be very insignificant circumstances ; but so it was, as appears from the account he gives of how they came about.

"It is rather curious, at least to me," he says, "that it was by a *picture* that I was first led to take an interest in Ragged Schools, a picture in an old, obscure, decaying burgh, that stands on the shore of the Firth of Forth. I had gone thither with a companion on a pilgrimage ; not that there was any beauty about the place, for it had no beauty. It has little trade ; its deserted harbour, silent streets, and old houses, some of them nodding to their fall, give indications of decay. But one circumstance has redeemed it from obscurity, and will preserve its name to the latest ages. It was the birthplace of Thomas Chalmers. I went to see the place (it is many years ago), and going into an inn for refreshments, I found the room covered with pictures of shepherdesses with their crooks, and tars in holiday attire, not very interesting. But above the chimney-piece there stood a large print, more respectable than its neighbours, which the skipper, the captain of one of the few ships that trade between that town and England, had probably brought there. It represented a cobbler's room; the cobbler was there himself, spectacles on his nose, an old shoe between his knees, that massive forehead and firm mouth expressing great determination of character, and below his bushy eyebrows benevolence gleamed out on a number of poor ragged boys and girls, who stood at their lessons around the busy cobbler. My curiosity was excited, and in the inscription I read how this man, John Pounds, a cobbler in Portsmouth, taking pity on the poor ragged children, left by ministers and magistrates, and ladies and gentlemen, to run the streets, had, like a good shepherd, gathered in the wretched outcasts; how he had brought them to God and the world; and how, while earning his bread by the sweat of his brow, he had rescued from misery, and saved to society, not less than five hundred of these children. I felt ashamed of myself for the little I had done."

Subsequently Dr. Guthrie paid a visit to the town of Portsmouth, and while there he says, " I went to a place I have great interest in, St. Mary's Street. I went along that street till I came to a very humble part of the town. I paused at the shop of the man in whose history I felt so deep an interest. I went into the shop. It was a cobbler's shop. I think it was about ten feet long and seven wide, and there worked the poor cobbler. Before that man was laid in his grave he was the means of saving not fewer than five hundred children from eternal ruin, and making them useful members of society; and he did that without fee or reward, without praise, without pay, without notice; but that man has run into celebrity since he was laid in his grave. The man I refer to was John Pounds, the founder of Ragged Schools. There was a poor cobbler who had his shop running over with children. He was to get nothing for it. Yet he used to entice the boys to come in; and if a boy happened to be Irish, he might have been seen holding a smoking potato under the urchin's nose in order to get him to come to school."

Such an incident clearly teaches that we should never despise small opportunities, or feeble means, if we wish to accomplish any good in the world; inasmuch as, in all directions, we can find how true it is, that if we want a field in which to labour, we can find it anywhere.

Again, when speaking of the circumstances by which he was induced to give his attention to the Temperance cause, and in which he was able to accom-

plish so much good, he says, "I take peculiar interest
in the cabmen, whom I take to be second cousins to
the carmen of Ireland, to one of whom, in a good
measure, I owe it that I am an abstainer. It is
twenty-two years since I first visited Ireland. I went
with Mr. C. J. Brown and Mr. Bridges as a
deputation. In this journeying we reached a town
called Omagh, whence we had to travel through
a mountainous country to another place called Cocton.
The day was one of the worst possible, with bitter cold
and lashing rain. Half-way there stood a small inn,
into which we went, as a sailor in stress of weather
runs into the first haven. These were the days, not
of toast and tea, but when it was thought that the
best cure for a wet coat and of a cold body was a
tumbler of toddy, and we no sooner got within the
inn than the toddy was ordered. We took our toddy,
and, no doubt, in moderation. But if we, with all our
wraps on, were in an uncomfortable state, far more
uncomfortable was our half-ragged carman; if we
were drenched, he was drowned. Of course, we felt
for our courteous and civil driver, and we thought
what was sauce for the goose was sauce for the
gander, and we offered him a glass; but the carman
was not such a gander as we, like geese, took him
for; to our perfect amazement, not one drop of the
toddy would he touch. He said, "I am an abstainer,
and will take no toddy." Well, that stuck in my
throat, and it went to my heart and (though in another

sense than drink) to my head. That and other circumstances made me a teetotaler."

It was in the old, quiet Scottish burgh of Brechin that Thomas Guthrie was born, on the 12th of July, 1803, and it was there he chiefly spent the first twenty-seven years of his life. In his writings he indicates what a strong hold the place had on his affections to the last. Every year he visited it several times, and enjoyed the kindly welcome and salutations which he always received from group after group as he met them. Among other things he says, "I remember when a boy there was not a working man who had a watch. There were only two gold watches, and they were the wonder of the place ; but now the working men have all their watches."

He was the twelfth child, and the sixth son, of David Guthrie. His mother's maiden name was Clementina Cay. Thirteen children were born to them, of whom ten grew up. It is impossible to overstate the influence which his mother exercised over him. He never spoke of her but with profound reverence ; nor is this to be wondered at when, as one says, he was not unmindful of the source from which he and his family originated, as may be gathered from the following statement. "Through my ancestors, so far as I can trace them," said Dr. Guthrie when writing about his forefathers, "I can claim to be the seed of the righteous, a higher honour than the 'blue blood' some boast of, though why noble blood should be called 'blue' which is venous or polluted blood, I have yet to learn."

Like many other noble men, he could trace much of the influence which governed his life to his mother. The following is his own testimony :—

"It was at my mother's knee that I first learned to pray; there I learned to form a reverence for the Bible as the inspired Word of God, that I learned to hold the sanctity of the Sabbath, that I learned the peculiarities of the Scottish religion, that I learned my regard to the principles of civil and religious liberty, which have made me hate oppression, and whether it be a pope, or a prelate, or a patron, or an ecclesiastical demagogue, I resist the oppressor."

While yet an infant he had quite a serious illness, and was brought back, very unexpectedly, from the very gates of death, and when a boy he had a narrow escape from death by accident, when wading across a swollen river with another boy on his back. Getting dizzy and falling off, the boy lost his presence of mind, and striking out with his hands and feet, and bellowing like a madman as he lay floating, fast in the grip of Guthrie, on the top of the flood. It was with the utmost difficulty they both were able to reach the shore.

On another occasion, during his ministry at Arbirlot, he went down to the sea-side among the rocks at Arbroath when the waves were running, as it is said, "mountains high," and missed his footing. That very day he had fortunately had the heels of his boots armed with iron, and it came to his mind like a flash of lightning that by pressing his heels firmly he might catch against a piece of the rock and be saved ; he did so, and was plucked from the jaws of death as by a miracle.

On another occasion, while playing with his brother Charles with a gun, not knowing it was loaded, and snapping the flint and pointing it at each other, to their horror it went off, but fortunately the charge lodged deep in a wall.

Books for the young were comparatively scarce when Dr. Guthrie was a boy. Almost the only one interesting to the young mind was the " Pilgrim's Progress." But, as he adds, the case is so different now, that "with the variety and piquancy and attractiveness of books nowadays, provided for Sabbath use, there is no excuse for people, whether old or young, seeking relaxation in museums or public gardens or Sunday excursions, or saying that the Sabbath is a weariness, and wishing it were over. As for the plea set up for Sabbath walks and excursions for the sake of health by the working classes, there is no truth in it. If women would spend less on finery and men on whisky and tobacco, they could spare an hour or two every day for more than all the relaxation which health requires ; Sabbath keepers have happier homes and longer lives than Sabbath breakers."

When only four years old he was sent to what might be called an infants' school ; the fees were helpful to the teacher, a good Christian man. Having learnt his letters, and some small words printed on a fly-sheet of the Shorter Catechism, he was then passed into the Book of Proverbs, which was the usual method in those days, and one which it would have been well never to have given up. Speaking of this in after life, Dr. Guthrie says, " That book is without a rival for beginners, containing quite a repository of monosyllables and pure Saxon 'English undefiled.' . . . . While learning the art of reading by that Book of Proverbs, we had our minds stored with the highest moral truths ; and, by sage advices applicable to all the ages and departments of life, the branch, while it was supple, received a bent in a direction highly favourable to future well-doing and success in life." The patience, prudence, foresight, economy which mark the " canny Scotch," and which so often help them to rise in the world, he says, are largely due to their thus being engrained in youth and childhood with the practical wisdom enshrined in the Book of Proverbs.

At the age of twelve he had to leave home for college. Speaking of the time when he had thus to start out for a city he had never seen, and where one day he was to be known so well, he says, " That eventful morning when we first left a father's house, and as the gates of that happy sanctuary slowly opened

for our departure, amid tears and many a kind farewell, watched by a father's anxious eye, and followed
by a mother's prayers, we pushed out our bark on the
swell of life's tempestuous sea. That day, the turning-
time of many a young man's history, the crisis of his
destiny, may have exerted an influence as permanent
on our fate as its impression remains indelible in our
memory." It was no easy task to accomplish in those
days. There were no steamboats, railways, and only
few stage coaches. Lads were very glad of a life
in a carrier's cart to help them on their way. His
lodgings, including cost for coals, attendance, and cook-
ing, only came to 5s. or 6s a week ; the usual fare for
living was tea once, oatmeal porridge twice a day,
and for dinner, fresh herrings and potatoes. Butchers'
meat only was indulged in about twice during the
whole of the first session at college. No wonder, he
tells us, that " six of us had a common table, and we
used to make up for the outlay of occasional suppers by
dinners of potatoes and ox livers, which we reckoned
cost us only three half-pence a head. Sydney Smith,"
he adds, " might joke about a Scotsman cultivating
the arts and sciences on oatmeal, but the struggle
which many an ambitious lad makes to fight his way
on through college is a feather in the cap of our
country." It will thus be seen he was not ashamed
to own the humble position and honest struggles of
his early days.

Like another eminent man who rose from a very

humble position (Dr. Carey, the famous missionary)
Dr. Guthrie believed in the importance of plodding,
"the genius of plod." On one occasion he said, " I
would remind you that there is no royal road to
knowledge ; all must work to learn knowledge as well
as to learn trades ; learning is only to be got by work,
and·you may think me rather professional, but I will
give you an illustration how difficulties are got over
by hard perseverance. A minister who had got no
memory was asked how he was able to get his sermons
by heart. 'Why,' replied he, 'I just sit down
doggedly to it.' The young men who attend these
apprentice schools must just do the same ; for, as Sir
Joshua Reynolds said, 'it is not given to man to
attain excellence in anything but as the effect of
labour.' Some young men believe they have genius ;
but I believe every man of genius on this platform
will agree with me, that the finest genius is like
the richest soil, if you do not manure it, it will
run out. If knowledge cannot accumulate in the
mind, a man will soon find himself at the end of
his thread."

Before he was sixteen he had finished his four
years' curriculum of literature and philosophy, and
left college at the age when most youths nowadays are about entering it. Among other things for
which he was thankful, he says, " My father was
prudent enough to keep me very short of money, and
always required me, at the close of the session, on my

return home. to account for every penny I received.
And for this, which I may have thought hard at the
time, I now bless his memory." Altogether it took
him eight years to run his college course, and two
additional years before he was licensed to preach, and
after that he was five years before he obtained a
presentation to a church. Fifteen years of his life
were spent at no small cost ; and even then he had a
"_starving_" rather than a _living_, as he calls a minister's
profession.

Meantime he had to enter the bank, in which he
passed " two busy but not lost years." He considered
these as not the least valuable part of his training and
education.

Once, when speaking in Dundee, he referred to
these early struggles in the following graphic manner.
" I don't intend to give you any learned discussion on
commerce. The truth is, that is rather out of my line,
and I won't meddle with it in that way ; not that I
am altogether ignorant of commerce, either. I don't
want any of you to understand that I was a banker
two years, and Mr. David Milne, formerly of the
Union Bank, said when I left that profession (for if
nobody will praise me I must praise myself), that if I
preached as well as I banked, I would get on remarkably well ; so you see I am not so ignorant of
these things as one of my brethren with whom I was
sitting one day. He took up a newspaper and began
reading ; when he came upon 'Sound' intelligence,

which you Dundee people all know means the ships
that pass through the 'Sound,' 'Why,' says he,
"what do they mean by Sound? Is it intelligence
that may be relied on?"

Nor was his knowledge confined to this subject, as
he plainly goes on to say, "Neither am I so ignorant
of agricultural affairs. At least I have been in the
habit of testing the agricultural knowledge of my
brethren in the Church by asking them how many
teeth a cow has in her front upper jaw, and they don't
know a bit about it; they don't know that a cow has
no teeth in her front upper jaw at all. Some of them
guessed half-a-dozen, and some of them a whole dozen.
They were all as ignorant as an old friend of mine in
the city of Brechin, who wished to have a first-rate cow.
He accordingly gave £12 or £15 for a handsome
one, thinking that she was in the flush of her milk and
the beauty of her youth. But a wag went up to him
afterwards and said to him, "Dear me, look, Mr.
Smith, she hasna a tooth in her upper jaw. You have
been fairly taken in. Instead of buying a young milk
cow, she is a venerable grandmother."

On the 13th of May, 1830, he was ordained the
minister of Arbirlot; five months after, he married the
lady to whom he had been engaged for some years.
It might have seemed to the aspiring mind of the
ardent young man like going out "into the wilderness"
to be sent to that small seaside village rather than
to the greater work and larger responsibilities which

afterwards came upon him. But it proved, as such places have often done before, that obscurity is the best training ground for the world's prophets, teachers, leaders, and worthies. One thing we do know, so far as Guthrie was concerned, he learnt lessons by that sea-shore, while watching its thousand aspects during those seven years, which can be traced everywhere in his writings and speeches. As we look at those pictures of real beauty and grandeur, we feel we are kept constantly in sight and hearing of the sea, and that they are the reproduction of mind of one who has often watched and waited for the lessons they suggest.

There are times in the history of most men, when they are called upon to take their stand against what they know and feel to be wrong, let the consequences be ever so serious to their own welfare and comfort. Happy is it for that man, and well it is for that nation, when such a bold and firm stand is taken, and they are ready to bid defiance to what they deem to be the forces of evil. Dr. Guthrie had to do this on several occasions. Speaking of this kind of experience he remarked, "I have had enough of fighting in my day. I thought I was done with it. I look upon it as a serious calamity when the civil and church courts come into collision. We may come to yield to what we think wrong in spiritual matters. I have no desire to be placed in the position I was before, when, in going to preach at Strathbogie, I was met by an

B

interdict from the Court of Session, an interdictto
which, as regards civil matters, I gave implicit
obedience. The better the day the better the deed, it
is said ; and on the Lord's Day, when I was preparing
for Divine Service, in came a servant of the law, and
handed me an interdict. I told him he had done his
duty, and I would do mine. I was present with Dr.
Cunningham and Dr. Candlish in the Court of
Session, and saw the presbytery of Dunkeld brought
to the bar for breach of interdict, and I heard the
Lord President of the Court of Session say, that on
the next occasion when the ministers broke the interdict they would be visited with all the penalties of the
law. The penalties of the law were to get lodgings
free gratis in Calton jail. That was my position on
that Sabbath morning. That interdict forbade me,
under the penalty of Calton jail, to preach the Gospel
in the parish church of Strathbogie. I said, the parish
churches are stone and lime, and belong to the State ;
I will not preach there. It forbade me to preach the
Gospel in the school-houses. I said, the school-houses
are stone and lime, and belong to the State ; I will
not preach there. It forbade me to preach in the
churchyard. I said, the dust of the dead is the
State's ; I will not preach there. But when those
Lords of Session forbade me to preach my Master's
blessed Gospel and offer salvation to sinners anywhere
in that district under the arch of heaven, I put that
interdict under my foot, and I preached the Gospel.

I defied them to punish me, and I have not been punished down to this day."

It is impossible not to admire the courage and fidelity to conscience with which Dr. Guthrie separated himself from his church and congregation, rather than swerve from the path of duty, especially when it is remembered that he was at the time in the receipt of £600 a year. This, however, he calmly resigned without a murmur, and gave up without remorse. It must have been a deep conviction which led him to take this step, or he would not have said, "I am no longer minister of St. John's. I understand that this day there has been a great slaughter in the Old Assembly, and among the rest my connection with the Established Church has been cut, or rather, I may say, *I have cut it myself.* I know they have resolved to declare my church vacant. *They may save themselves the trouble.*" Noble words, and a striking testimony to the courage of the man, giving, as it does, a clear indication that he was made of that kind of material which, alas! is not too plentiful in this world, but of which it would be well for the world if it could secure a larger supply, and turn it to as good an account, as subsequent events in the history of Scotland amply furnished proof.

It is often found that those people who do little or nothing to benefit their fellows themselves are very apt to cover their own defects, by charging others with being "crotchety," "men of one idea," or "carried

away with a hobby," and so on; but careful inquiry
will invariably result in its being seen that those who
are earnest about one thing are generally earnest about
other subjects which they find obstructs the general
well-being of the people.   It was so with Dr. Guthrie.
While his name is associated in some minds with the
work of ragged schools, it is also identified with others—
with that of the great movement in which he and 500
others left the Church of their fathers, rather than
sacrifice the sacred rights of conscience; preferring
rather to thus suffer with the people of God than to
live in luxury, by surrendering their convictions at the
shrine of worldly patronage.   To some people, however, he is better known as an ardent Temperance
advocate, both in and out of his pulpit, where also
he was noted alike for his eloquence, power, and
success.

It may naturally be asked why Dr. Guthrie was
such a warm advocate of Temperance, and so determined an enemy to the liquor traffic.   Let us hear
what he has to say himself: "Seven years of my
ministry were spent in one of the lowest localities of
Edinburgh, and it almost broke my heart day by day
to see, as I wandered from house to house and from
room to room, misery, wretchedness, and crime; the
detestable vice of drunkenness, the cause of all, meeting me at every turn, and marring all my efforts.   If
there is one thing I feel more intensely than
another it is this, that drinking is our national curse,

our sin and shame, our weakness. I speak the words of truth and soberness when I say that this vice destroys more men and women, bodies and souls, breaks more hearts, ruins more families than all other vices put together. Nor need I speak of the multitude of lives it costs. Nothing ever struck me more, in visiting these wretched localities, than to find that more than half of these families were in the churchyard. The murder of innocent infants by drunkenness out-Herods Herod in his slaughter of the innocents of Bethlehem. I appeal to every missionary and every minister who visits these localities, whether the great obstacle that meets him at every corner is not drunkenness. I believe we will in vain plant churches and schools, though they be as thick as trees in the forest, unless this evil is stopped." .

Dr. Guthrie was once travelling in the Highlands of Scotland with his wife. Speaking afterwards of that visit, he says : " We ought to show sympathy for the poor Highlanders ; but I am sorry to say I saw too much evidence of drinking. I remember that at the inn where we were staying we were very much disturbed by the rioting and noises of some drunken parties. On one occasion the door opened, and in came a fellow reeling, and most uncommonly polite— for the Highlander is polite, even when he is in drink. He bowed, and called me 'My lord,' which I am not, and Mrs. Guthrie 'My lady,' and was bowing and scraping in the most polite style, when in came the servant girl, and, taking him by the shoulders, turned him out with a dexterity which showed she was well accustomed to that kind of thing. Drink is a curse to the Lowlands, and to the Highlands too."

It requires a great deal of moral courage to stand alone, but Dr. Guthrie was evidently not wanting in that commodity. "I remember," says he, "very well the first great party I went to with the resolution of making my first appearance as a teetotaler. It required almost as much courage on my part as I would have required to go up to a battery of cannon. Nevertheless, *I did what I thought was my duty*, and I rather delighted to go in such a capacity, for this reason : that I had a good opportunity of practically exhibiting the principles of total abstinence, and if there happened to be somebody present who did attack me, I rejoiced to have an opportunity of pummelling him."

That he was able to make good his position at all times may be readily inferred if we take into account what he was in the habit of calling his four good reasons for being an abstainer. "My head is clearer, my health is better, my heart is lighter, and my purse is heavier ;" and to a man having so much to do as he had, a clear head, a sound body, a light heart, and a full purse were no small advantages.

Dr. Guthrie was once invited to speak at a temperance meeting, when he gave the following portrait of himself, much to the amusement of the audience:

" I am not come," he said, " for the purpose of speaking, and I can assure you that I will not trespass upon
your time ; and indeed I would not have come, but it
being a total abstinence meeting, I wished to give it my
countenance, although I am afraid that this will be of
very little benefit to you. A friend of mine has told
me that a person who was asked to describe Dr.
Guthrie said that he was a hard-favoured man, with a
voice like thunder. I am therefore afraid that his
countenance will not do you much good."

Sometimes he vindicated his practice in the following manner :—" I am not a teetotaler because I
was coming to like the drink, as a lady supposed who
said to Dr. Miller, ' I am sorry Dr. Guthrie has got to
bad habits, and has been obliged to become a member
of the teetotal society to keep him from being
deposed.' "

At other times he would humorously give some
of his reasons in favour of water drinking in the following way :—" I could stand here from morning to
sundown, and from sundown to sunrise, occupying, if
I had physical power, every hour and every minute of
that time telling the evil these stimulants have done,
and I will defy any man to occupy five minutes by
telling me the good they have done. Everybody
knows I have been talking everlastingly all the winter
through. I have done, I believe, double the amount
of public work of that of any minister in Edinburgh, and yet people have said to me ' You

are looking remarkably well; you are looking ten
years younger. How is that?' 'Cold water' is my
answer."

Dr. Guthrie was one of the founders of the Free
Church Temperance Society, and he also assisted in
the formation of the Scottish Society for the Sup-
pression of Drunkenness. In connection with that
society he published their first tract, entitled "A Plea
on behalf of Drunkards, and against Drunkenness,"
and other tracts. In 1857 he published "The
City: its Sins and Sorrows," which created a profound sensation. Over 50,000 copies have been
circulated.

The following extract from this book illustrates
very vividly what a deep hold the lives of little
ragged children had upon his sympathy :—

"Look," he says, "look at the case of a boy whom
I saw lately. He was but twelve years of age, and
had been seven times in gaol. The term of his im-
prisonment was run out, and so he had doffed his
prison garb and resumed his own. It was the depth
of winter, and having neither shoes nor stockings, his
red naked feet were upon the frozen ground. Had
you seen him shivering in his scanty dress, the misery
pictured on an otherwise comely face, the tears that
dropped over his cheeks as the child told his pitiful
story, you would have forgotten that he was a thief,
and only seen before you an unhappy creature, more
worthy of a kind word, a loving look, a helping hand,

than the guardianship of a turnkey and the dreary solitude of a gaol.

"His mother was in the grave. His father had married another woman. They both were drunkards. Their den, which is in the High Street—I know the place—contained one bed, reserved for the father, his wife, and one child. No couch was kindly spread for this poor child and his brother—a mother's son, then also immured in gaol. When they were fortunate enough to be allowed to be at home, their only bed was the hard, bare floor. I say fortunate enough, because on many a winter night their own father hounded them out. Ruffian that he was, he drove his infants weeping from the door, to break their young hearts and bewail their cruel lot on the corner of some filthy stair, and sleep away the cold, dark hours as best they could, crouching together for warmth like two houseless dogs."

That it is very much easier to be a teetotaler nowadays than it was in Thomas Guthrie's youthful times, may be gathered from the following account, where he says : " When I was a student, there was not, I believe, an abstaining student within the University, and not one abstaining minister in the whole Church. I did, indeed, know one minister who was practically a total abstainer, but my worthy friend's total abstainence was because he thought he could not stand drinking." On another occasion he said : " A minister of the Gospel, a clever man in

his way, said to another friend of mine the other day,
'Become a total abstainer? Is there any reason why
I should have my hands tied behind my back in case
I should fight?' This is not a fair analogy. The
ground I take up is that the mischief the drink does
is so many thousand times greater than the good it
does, that on the principles of Christian expediency
and love of humanity, men should give it up. 'Tie
your hands behind your back' is not an analogous
case at all. Here is an analogous case. You see a
man going about with a long beard. Some say that
long beards are good for preventing colds and chest
complaints, therefore the beard is a very good thing.
Now, the truth is, I see my friends with beards strok-
ing them with manifest delight, so that it is plain it
is not the danger of cold, but because they think them
ornamental, that they wear them. Supposing the
beard shaving to go on as it does, and every tenth
man who used the razor to cut his throat—supposing
that, what would you say? I would preach in favour
of beards from the pulpit. I say it would be the duty
of every man to wear a beard, and never to handle a
razor, if it could be proved and demonstrated that
every tenth man that handled a razor cut his throat.
If I can prove that something like the same proportion of evil is done by the use of strong drink, that
something like the same proportion destroys by it
character, household comfort, domestic happiness, and bodies and souls, is there a man

among us that would not say, 'Be done with drinking?'"

At a dinner-party his wine-glass stood untouched before him. A lady noticing this, said, " Doctor, why don't you take your wine?" He replied, "I do not care for it." "Are you unwell?" "Oh, no!" "Then why not take it?" "Well, I don't want it." "Doctor," said another lady, "I see your wine is standing. untouched." "I know it." "Why not take it?" "Well, the fact is I am a teetotaler." "Dear me, Doctor, I never heard you were a drunkard!" "Nor have I been one, but in my visitations through the closes and alleys of Edinburgh, seeing the evils that drink is doing, I thought it was more my place instead of saying *go* and be a teetotaler, to say *come* and be a teetotaler."

At another time he said : "I have thought it would be a capital plan if any of you who have saved money by going to the Corn Exchange instead of the public-house—and I am sure that many in this house have done so—would give that saving to me for the purpose I have indicated, I am sure it would be a ten thousand times softer pillow to lie on to think that you had given a shilling or a sixpence, and to know that you had done something to save a child from ruin, than to lie next morning with what the man called a ' rivin ' headache."

Replying to an objector once, he remarked :—" I would rather see in the pulpit a man who is a total abstainer from this root of all evil—drink—than a man crammed with all the Hebrew roots in the world." So firmly assured was he of. the ultimate prevalence of the principles of temperance that he went so far as to say on one occasion that "in the course of another generation the man who shall sit down to his bottle of wine or his tumbler of toddy will be as rare as those creatures, the Megatheriums, which remain to us the strange specimens of another and, let us be thankful, a past generation."

Nor was he without good reasons for these opinions, as may be gathered from the following illustration, where he says : "When you get religion dying, drink is like a fungus growing upon a rotten tree. When religion begins to revive, along with it revive temperance and total abstinence societies. There is a remarkable connection. The moment a revival appeared, in many places the public-houses began to shut up.

"I have before me a number of young men, who, in God's providence, are not only to tell on the rising generation, but who are to be placed in the most influential positions which any man could occupy—to influence effectually the community. I look upon one divinity student as worth a hundred old grey-haired ministers. The reason why I set them above the ministers is just because the large body of the ministers are advanced in life. So I look upon such divinity students as are before me as the best recruits that can be got in the cause of temperance. I have great pleasure in seeing so many men who care to fill the pulpits of our country, and mould the habits of the rising generation in our beloved land, in favour of total abstinence, and this all the more when I look back on the old divinity students. I don't say that the students of that day were dissolute and immoral men : far from it There were black sheep among them, no doubt. Even among divinity students there were suppers, and if there were suppers there were tumblers, and if there were tumblers there was toddy, and I don't know, in regard to them, whether, as there were tumblers, there was tumbling ; but it was a very likely thing."

It may be encouraging to some timid beginners to know that one who became so famous as a pulpit orator did not at first appear to realise his own gifts. When once asked what his own opinion was, he frankly said : "I always feel greatly dissatisfied with my own performance ; though, at the same time, when I heard some others preach, ' Well,' thought I to myself, ' I could do better than that.' " In a letter he wrote to a young minister respecting his own first sermon, he said : " I remember when I broke ground at Dun leaving the Church happy that I had not stuck. I thought that was a great step, a great achievement, and that now, having got a beginning made, I would by-and-by get in with the rest. I remember being troubled in a way you don't seem to have felt. I did not know exactly what to do with my hands. I would have felt it to be a great relief if I could, consistently with decorum, have put them in my pockets! As to my eyes, I don't know how I managed with them."

It is a grand thing to believe in *possibility*—to have the conviction that something can be done to make the world better, and that as sure as we act in harmony with its promptings we shall succeed. Such, evidently, was Dr. Guthrie's idea when he observed, in urging the claims of the ragged children :—" Keeping out of view the depravity of human nature which is common to all, these (ragged) children are very much what you choose to make them. The soul of that ragged boy or girl is like a mirror. Frown upon it, and it frowns upon you. Look at it with suspicion, and it eyes you in the same manner. Lift your arm to strike, and there is an arm lifted against you. Turn your back, and it turns its back on you. Turn round and give it a smile, and it smiles again in return. It will give smile for smile, kindness for kindness."

In illustration of this, he tells us that one day he was asked to come downstairs. On doing so, he found some girls who were about to be sent out abroad by a society which had been formed for that purpose. He found that they had got over the fears they once had entertained upon the subject, and were then ready to proceed to their distant home. "Along with the girls," he says, " I saw a boy, the brother of one of them, who had come to Edinburgh to bid her farewell, and commit her to the care of God. He was a remarkably fine-looking lad, a pretty shepherd boy. He looked as if he had never snuffed the smoke of Edinburgh before. You may fancy, when I saw him standing before me, a plaid across his breast, a bonnet on his head, long yellow locks flowing over his shoulders, shoes on his feet fitted to stand the wear of the heather, and in his hand a shepherd's staff, and two as pretty roses blooming on his cheeks as ever you saw, you may imagine how my heart leapt with joy when I was told : ' That's one of your Ragged School boys.'"

On another occasion he gave the history of a real hero in the following graphic manner :—" We have ragged scholars that are cutting down the forests in America. We have them herding sheep in Australia. We have them in the navy ; and what do you think ? There was an odd thing in this way : we had a competition among boys in the navy, and the Ragged School boys carried off the highest prizes. We have them in the army too. Just the other day I had in my drawing-room one of my ragged scholars. What was he doing there ? you ask. Well, he was just standing beside a very pretty girl, dressed like a duchess, with an enormous crinoline, and all that. There he was, and on his breast he carried three medals. He had fought the battles of his country in

the Crimea. He had also gone up the deadly march to
Lucknow, and rescued the women, and the children,
and the soldiers there. And was I not proud of my
Ragged School boy when I saw him with his
honours !"

Take another illustration to which he referred
with equal joy. "One of our boys, a very little
fellow, but uncommonly smart, entered the lists, and
carried off a prize against the whole of England and
Scotland by his answer to the question, 'Give the
history of the Apostle Paul in thirty words ?' Now
listen to the answer. It looks like as if it had gone
through a Bramah press, it is so well condensed :—
Paul was born at Tarsus, and brought up at Jerusalem. He continued a persecutor till his conversion,
after which he became a follower of Christ, for whose
sake he died.' Now, could any of you have done half
so well ?"

When sixty-five years of age, and while reviewing
his past life, Dr. Guthrie said : " People should shine
as lights in the world, but not put the candle in a
draught or doorway. It is better, no doubt, as they
say, to wear out than to rust out ; but the weights of
a clock may be made so heavy as to damage the
machinery, and make it run down before its proper
time. We have no more right to shorten our own than
another's life, and the duty of self-preservation which
instinct teaches is one which the Bible enforces. A
knowledge of the ordinary rules of health ought, there-

fore, to be regarded as one of the most useful branches of education; and considering how easily they may be acquired, and how many diseases are spread and lives lost through the neglect of them, it is astonishing that they are not taught in all our schools. Were these rules learned to be practised, and were people to observe moderation in all things—abstaining especially from every cup stronger than that which cheers, but not inebriates—and were our working classes as well fed, clothed, and housed as they might be were they to abstain from the use of expensive and dangerous luxuries, thousands of lives would be saved, thousands of accidents and diseases avoided, and the three-score years and ten would probably prove not the ordinary limit, but the ordinary average of human life—as many living beyond that period as died before it."

"Remember," he said on another occasion, "this world is not for enjoyment; it is for employment. This earth is not for wages, but for work. Earth for the work, heaven for the wages. Earth for employment, heaven for enjoyment. Earth for toil, heaven for rest."

In March, 1872, his health began to fail. On August 25th he preached his last sermon from the text, "The just shall live by faith." Gradually he sank, and about ten o'clock on the Sabbath, February 23rd, 1873, he fell into a broken sleep, and a few hours after quietly passed away to the better land. He

c

was interred, amid the most impressive demonstration ever known in Edinburgh, on the 28th of February in the Grange Cemetery. All over the world the news of his death was received with profound grief by every one who had any knowledge of his works of faith and labours of love It may not be without interest to say, that among other things which gave interest to his life is the fact that, holding as he did such sentiments as we have briefly sketched, and living with such a firm desire to be of some service to his fellow-men, it is not surprising to find that Dr. Guthrie was in the habit of expressing his convictions in strong and emphatic terms. Among the most favourite of the quotations with which he was wont to press home his appeals were these words :—

> " I live for those who love me,
>   For those who know me true ;
> For the heaven that smiles above me,
>   And awaits my spirit too ;
> For the wrong that needs resistance,
> For the cause that lacks assistance,
> For the future in the distance,
>   And the good that I can do."

May the young readers of these pages be imbued with the same deep earnestness which distinguished the life of THOMAS GUTHRIE.

(Our Portrait of Dr. Guthrie is from a Photograph by J. Moffat, Edinburgh.)

FATHER MATHEW,

IRELAND'S APOSTLE OF TEMPERANCE.

ONE day, while Mrs. Mathew was sitting at the dinner table, surrounded by her large family of boys and girls, she exclaimed, as with not a little natural mother's pride she looked at her army of handsome, healthy boys, "Is it not unfortunate? I have nine sons, and not one of them to be a priest!" The boys glanced at George, who had been "intended" for that office, but he simply blushed and fixed his eyes steadily upon his plate, as if he did not wish to notice what had been said. The silence, however, was soon broken by Theobald starting from his chair, and saying, with a voice full of emotion, "Mother, don't be uneasy, I will be a priest." His mother expressed her delight by folding him in her arms, and covering him with kisses, while she in other ways manifested her gratitude and delight. From that moment his influence over his brothers, which had been very great before, became even more recognised, and gathered strength as the years rolled by, though, strange to say two of them became distillers, while he was equally well known all over the world as the Apostle of Temperance.

As a child, Theobald Mathew manifested many of the features which marked his character as a man. From his earliest days nothing seemed so natural to him as the desire to make others happy, or to give them pleasure. What at first was a mere habit in the child became the ruling passion of the man. From the day of his birth, which took place on the 18th of October, 1790, at Thomastown House, near Cashel, in Tipperary, he was the favourite child of his mother. There was something so sweet and engaging in him, that it drew his mother's heart towards him, while his love for her was manifested in a hundred child-like ways. The result was, that by his brothers and sisters he was scornfully called "the Pet," because he preferred sitting by his mother's side, rather than passing the time away in play with them. Young "Toby," as he was called, was rather averse to the rude sports in which they liked to engage, and though his brothers frequently accused him of "being tied to his mother's apron-strings," yet they had to own, that if they wanted any special indulgence from their mother, he was always ready to coax from her any little thing which would aid them in their enjoyment. Nothing gave him more pleasure than to see the relish with which they despatched some of the sweet morsels he was able to secure for them from time to time.

Among other things in which Theobald also delighted was plum-pudding. He used to tell a story how that on one Christmas he quietly hid beneath the cushion of a great old-fashioned chair the silver spoons which had been used with the plum-pudding. Great was the surprise of all the servants at the unaccountable - disappearance of the plate. No one seemed to know what to think of the matter. All at once Theobald confessed, with some pride, that he had put them away in a safe place, so that they might be ready at hand when the next Christmas came with its customary pudding. The result was that instead of waiting for Christmas, which was then, of course, a year distant, the young favourite was promised a plum-pudding every Sunday, a promise which was hailed with a shout of delight, as may be readily imagined.

Although he had three brothers older than himself, it was singular how he seemed to lead them, as if by natural right. They obeyed him as a matter of course. There was a something about him which drew them towards him, and led them to feel he was born to lead. He was never known to have uttered a bad word, or even one of doubtful meaning, and a harsh or unkind word was never known to have dropped from his lips. Neatness and order, both in his dress and the arrangements of his home, always marked his life. To find anything out of its right place gave him annoyance, and offended his sense of order and regularity. A striking incident of this is given in his early age. One day he happened to see in the breakfast-parlour a pair of silk stockings on the back of a chair before the fire, where they had been placed to " air " before being worn. His disgust was such, that he took them off the chair, and flung them in the fire, where they were soon destroyed. A keen search was ordered to be made for the missing articles, every one wondering what had become of them. At last Toby was asked if he had seen them. "I did, and burned them too," was his reply. "Burned them! Why did you do such a thing, you bold boy?" was the next question. "They had no right to be in the breakfast-parlour : that was no place for them," he replied sturdily. "Toby is right," said Lady Elizabeth Mathew, his grand aunt ; "they should not have been put there." The loss of the stockings was recompensed by the lesson the servants had given them from the lips of the child, as her ladyship owned at the time.

Nor was Theobald deficient in either moral or physical courage when it was needed, though they might call him "Miss Molly" at home. He had heard from some source that there lived about half-a-dozen miles from his father's house a gentleman whose reputation was so bad, that more than one village gossip in the blacksmith's forge, or the kitchen hob, was willing to "take her Bible oath" that he was gifted with a tail, though his horns could not be seen, and therefore he was "the ould boy himself, all out." Many of the servants in the house fully believed these strange rumours, and they seized fast hold of the lad's imagination, so he resolved to try and see whether Mr.—— was such a really bad character. So one morning he started off early on his pony, and galloped away to the gentleman's house, and remained seated for hours on his pony's back, hoping to satisfy his curiosity, but he had his labour in vain. A few years after, however, he met the same gentleman, and had the opportunity of convincing himself that however bad he might be *inside*, he was no different from others *outside*.

When he reached the age of twelve, Lady Elizabeth, his constant friend, decided to educate him at her own cost. So she selected a school for him at Kilkenny, to which he was sent. But his love of home was so strong, that he yielded to an uncontrollable desire to see his parents and family during the Easter festivities, and without letting any one know he set out on foot, and walked between thirty and forty miles, and at the end of the day, footsore and tired, he arrived, and was received in the arms of his delighted mother, who could not hint a word of reproof as she clasped him to her breast.

Having passed through his preliminary studies, he was sent to the College at Maynooth, where he matriculated on the 18th of September, 1807; but he was not destined to finish his scholastic career there, inasmuch as, owing to his having violated one of its rules, and rather than run the risk of an expulsion, he left it in 1808. Had he gone through the usual course in the classes of the College, he might have become an ordinary priest, and even wore a bishop's mitre, but in all human probability the world would never have heard of the name of Father Mathew, the Apostle of Temperance. After leaving Maynooth, he went to Dublin, and on Easter Sunday, 1814, he was ordained, and his mother's long-cherished ambition for her beloved son to see him a priest was fulfilled.

He delivered his first sermon in his native county, at Kilfeacle. It so happened that he read and explained the Saviour's words, " that it is more difficult for a rich man to enter the kingdom of heaven than for a camel to pass through the eye of a needle." Among his hearers was a stout, rich village magnate, who was much struck by the young preacher saying that it was not the *possession* of riches that was wrong in the sight of God, but the way they were *used*. Meeting the preacher after the sermon, the gentleman said, " Father Mathew, I feel very much obliged to you for trying to squeeze *me* through the eye of a needle." The old gentleman was at that time fat enough even to have blocked up the Camel's Gate at Jerusalem. Father Mathew's first mission was in Kilkenny, and soon after his arrival there a striking change was visible. The Friary, as it was called, became crowded by the poor and rich. His fame spread rapidly, and his virtues were upon every tongue; his personal goodness and the sterling qualities of his heart, combined with his wonderful zeal for the spread of religion, became recognised as the main secret of his growing power for good. From there he went to Cork, where he was to become even more renowned as a temperance reformer.

His fame soon began to be noised abroad, and he might be seen from early morn till late at night engaged in his duties. To help him to discharge them better, he began to learn the Irish language. This enabled him to talk and listen to the natives with ease and comfort. One Sunday morning he had been attending to his duties from six o'clock until after ten, and as he had been also engaged up to eleven the previous night, he was both weary and hungry. Just as he was about to leave four sailors rolled in, and asked him to hear their confessions. "Why did you not come at a more seasonable hour?" he asked, for the moment feeling angry. "I can't hear you now; come in the morning." The sailors turned to go, when a poor woman quietly came and touched him, and said, "They may not come again, sir." This was enough, and running after the sailors, he succeeded in bringing them back, and heard their confessions. Not content with this, he gave them some breakfast, and then sent them on their way rejoicing. He afterwards thanked the poor woman "through whom," he said, "the Holy Ghost had spoken to him."

After he had been three years in Cork there was a terrible outbreak of malignant typhus fever. Father Mathew, among other things, wanted to ascertain how a young man was doing; so he climbed over a wall at five o'clock in the morning to gain the tidings, rather than disturb the keeper of the lodge and his family. The invalid who was thus so much the object of his interest lived for many years to tell the story.

Father Mathew was very remarkable for his use of time. His favourite proverb was, "*Take time by the forelock, for he is bald behind.*" To do this he generally rose about five o'clock, and sometimes, when needful, earlier. He seemed to have the right moment for everything. He was punctual to the minute in his appointments, and often surprised his friends with the amount of work he performed. One day he was asked how he managed to rise so early; he answered, as pointing to a workshop, "If I were a cooper, and bound to Mr.——, I should be up as early, so as to be at my work at the appointed time, and thus become pleasing to Mr.——, my master. But I have a higher calling, and I serve a better Master; and am I to be less desirous of pleasing that Master than I should be to satisfy Mr.——?"

His heart was full of sympathy with the poor, and he always treated them with tenderness and great respect. He used to say of them, "They will be as high in heaven as the highest in the land." Often he relieved their distress. He also delighted to help those who had seen better days when under a cloud, and he did it in such a way, that often it was not known even for years who had come to their relief. The clerk of his chapel, who frequently had to do these things, quaintly used to say, " Look, sir, here is my notion on the subject : if the streets of Cork were paved with gold, and if Father Mathew had entire control over them, and could do what he liked with them, there would not be a paving-stone in all Cork by the end of the year."

Ever on the look-out to do good, it was no wonder his power over the people became great. Said a lady one day to another of the priests : " Oh, Dr. Collins, I have just been listening to a sermon from Father Mathew, and I have been greatly edified." " My dear," answered the priest, " *his life is a sermon.*" This was strictly correct, and although keenly alive to wrong and insult, and to benefit and kindness, he ever endeavoured to act up to another of his favourite maxims : " *A pint of oil is better than a hogshead of vinegar.*" Although naturally excitable, he con- trolled his impulses, and, to use his own words, " he struggled hard with the bitterness of the moment," and gained the victory over self. The " oil " proved the peacemaker. He had all the qualities of a great heart, throbbing with the most tender, generous, and holy emotions.

After he had been about twelve years in Cork, he

had become most popular among every class and creed. As a preacher his reputation had been gradually advancing, mainly because he always avoided anything of a sectarian or bigoted spirit. For the orphan he specially laboured. "I never," he once said, "meet in the street a ragged child, asking me for charity in the name of God, that I do not think I see the infant Jesus with outstretched hands, and hear the petition for human mercy emanating from the lips of the Divinity."

Another passage from one of his charity sermons gives us, as it were, the key to his whole life. He says, "Mercy! heavenly mercy! Had the Deity never spoken, had He never revealed, by prophet or apostle, that mercy was His will, its innate excellence, the high honour it confers upon us, *the delicious, the ineffable pleasure we enjoy in its exercise,* would be sufficient to point out to us the necessity of this indispensable duty."

Of his untiring exertions during the terrible cholera visitation in 1832 we have not space to tell, except to say, that he threw himself into the midst of its peril with an unselfish devotedness which astonished every one. Where the plague raged in all its horrors, he might be seen going from house to house, administering help from his own resources, until he was left without a shilling. "Give, give, give," so he preached, and so he practised; and when he gave his last mite he gave it in the name

of God, confident that God would send him more
to give.

A lady was one day driving out of the chapel a
party of children, because they were making too much
noise. "Why are you driving those children out?"
he asked. "They were disturbing the congregation;
and I must say, Father Mathew, I wonder how you
can tolerate them going in and out as they do." "My
dear madam, you must remember the words of our
Divine Redeemer, who said, '*Suffer the little ones to
come unto me, and forbid them not, for of such is the
kingdom of Heaven.*' If they come from curiosity now,
they will come to pray another time; and you cannot
tell what impression is made upon the mind of the
very youngest child that enters the House of God."
The lady was perfectly satisfied, and never again
interfered.

He had wonderful success as a peacemaker, and
delighted in healing up breaches between families.
His visits under such circumstances were those of an
angel, and few could resist his pleadings. "I declare,"
said one after Father Mathew had left him, "I believe
that man has some extraordinary power about him.
I had not the best feeling towards him, on account of
something that annoyed me; but, sir, I do assure you
the moment he grasped me by the hand there was
an end to my anger. I can't tell what it is, but if
we lived in another age, I should be inclined to say
there was magic in it." To which the friend replied:

"Would that we had more of such magic and such magicians in these days!" Yes, the magic of kindness was never better manifested than in the life of Father Mathew, as he went about doing good to rich and poor, and in this way securing the confidence of all classes and creeds in the city where he laboured.

For some years he acted as one of the governors of the Cork Workhouse, where the scenes he witnessed and the sad stories he heard stirred his heart to its core. One of the Board of Governors with him was an earnest, honest Quaker, named William Martin— "the grandfather of the temperance cause," as he was called. Long before Father Mathew had even the slightest idea of taking any part in the movement, William Martin had made up his mind that of all others, Theobald Mathew was the man best suited to make it successful. He never failed, when a good opportunity occurred at the Board meeting, to remark, as some case of a more distressing character came up for consideration, "Strong drink is the cause of this." And having secured the sympathy of his hearer, he would add, "Oh, Theobald Mathew! if thou would only give thy aid, much good could be done in the city."

Few nowadays can understand the difficulties which stood in the way of these early pioneers of the Temperance movement. Most people regarded them as fanatics of the worst kind. Everybody believed in moderate drinking, while total abstinence was looked

upon as the dream of a madman, and downright
flying in the face of Providence. That was the kind
of argument, as it was called, with which they were
assailed. But still they persevered. Among the most
noted, in addition to William Martin, was the Rev.
Nicholas Dunscombe, a Protestant clergyman, and
Richard Dowden, a prominent member of the
Unitarian body. These, with a few working-men, did
the best they could, but being of a different religious
persuasion to the bulk of the people, their efforts were
regarded with the suspicion that something in the way
of proselytising was intended. The result was that
the cause made slow progress ; but still they worked
away, hoping better things.

" Oh, Theobald Mathew ! if *thou* would but take
the cause in hand," was the constant appeal of William Martin, "thou couldst do such good to these
poor creatures." These words haunted the kind and
tender heart of Father Mathew. But it was some
time ere he made any sign, though he was thinking
seriously of the subject. It was not until he was in the
forty-seventh year of his age that he solemnly began
to face it. He had witnessed the dreadful doings of
drink among all classes. To use his own words, "he
had seen the stars of heaven fall, and the cedars
of Lebanon laid low." In the prison, madhouse,
workhouse, hospital, everywhere he had gone, he
had met with its track marks. " But was not
religion sufficient to meet the evil?" "Had it not

produced greater results than this required?" But those addicted to drink did not come within the house of God. What *could* be done? he asked, as he sat in the midnight hour musing. Was there a remedy in the Total Abstinence movement? Would it, could it, ever be adopted to any extent to meet the case. Everything seemed against such a probability. Look at the social drinking customs of the people, the example of moderation which he and others had practised; think of the great fact that hundreds of people, including many of his own personal friends, were engaged in making and selling such drinks—what would become of them? these and a host of other inquiries crossed his mind, still the appeal came: "Oh, Theobald Mathew! if *thou* would only give thy aid, what good thou would do for these poor creatures." The responsibility was too awful, the risk too terrible, the possibilities of success too important, the shame of a failure too grave, to allow him to trifle with such convictions. In prayer, on his knees before God, he sought for guidance and counsel how to act and what to do. The answer came, and he arose convinced that, for the sake of the people, he ought boldly to join the crusade, and place himself in connection with the movement, and do all he could to advance it among the people. Having thus made up his mind, after long, careful, and prayerful deliberation, he resolved to act promptly. Like Cæsar, having crossed the Rubicon, he resolved to go forward.

So he decided to send at once for William Martin to come and see him.

It was in the month of April, 1838, that William Martin received a message from Father Mathew, asking him to call at his house in Cove Street that evening. Somehow William had a kind of idea that his long looked-for desire was about to be realised. At the appointed time he went, and was met at the door by Father Mathew, with a face radiant with kindness and good humour, with these words, " Welcome, Mr. Martin ; welcome, my dear friend. It is very kind of you to come to me at so short a notice, and so punctually too." To which the honest Quaker replied, " I was right glad to come to thee, Father Mathew, for I expected that thou had good news for me." " Well, Mr. Martin, I have sent for you to assist me in forming a Temperance Society in this neighbourhood." " I knew it !" said William. " Something seemed to tell me that thou would do it at last." It was decided by them to hold a meeting on the following Tuesday, and the good Quaker went on his way, exclaiming, " Oh, Father Mathew ! thou hast made me a happy man this night."

When it became known in Cork that Father Mathew had decided to take this step, many ridiculed the idea of his joining the " fanatics." Some said he had lost his senses ; others laughed and sneered. But the meeting, though a small one, was held. Father Mathew took the chair, and gave his reasons

D

for coming to such a conclusion, and then taking a pen to sign the pledge, he said, in a voice heard by all, and remembered by many for years after, " HERE GOES, IN THE NAME OF GOD, THEOBALD MATHEW, C.C., Cove Street, No. 1." Sixty others followed, including some who proved staunch friends to the promise, made that eventful night—the 10th April, 1838.

It is impossible to describe the joy of William Martin, and the satisfaction of others which followed that meeting. Nor did they for a moment dream of the extent to which its results would reach. Suffice it to say, that from that time Father Mathew became public property. Day by day he had to pass through an amount of work, both of body and mind, he never anticipated, or it might have appalled even his self-sacrificing spirit. In three months from that date 25,000 others had followed his example; in five months, 131,000; in less than nine months, 156,000 ; and long before he died more than 2,000,000 received the pledge at his hands; and although it is true much of this work proved very temporary in its character, yet, so long as it lasted, it was a clear gain to the cause of human welfare, and had it only lasted for a week, it would have been a profit of a week's sobriety, and that alone would have made it well worth the doing. With many thousands, however, it proved permanent, and there are valuable remains to be seen even now all over Ireland, England, and America, of the broad marks which Father

Mathew scored on the world's face, as the result of his apostolic labours.

Having thus started, Father Mathew had to go on. The result was that a new society, over which he was appointed president, was formed. At the second meeting 330 more names were added to the roll. The old school-room was soon found to be too small to accommodate the large numbers who flocked to the meetings, and the Horse Bazaar, a building capable of holding 4,000 persons, was at once rented for the purpose of the Temperance Association. It was there, that in a dimly-lighted building the Temperance cause was rocked and nursed, until it became a sturdy infant, and at length drew attention to what it was doing. Owing to the earnest appeals of Father Mathew and others who helped him, by January, 1839, the roll had increased to 200,000.

The following is a copy of the pledge which was taken :—

" I promise, with the Divine assistance, as long as I shall continue a member of the Teetotal Temperance Society, to abstain from all intoxicating drinks, except for medicine or sacramental puposes ; and to prevent as much as possible, by advice and example, drunkenness in others."

The movement rolled on with a mighty sweep from that time. Limerick was the first place he visited on his missionary labour. After four days' labour, 150,000 took the pledge at his hand. At Waterford in three days 80,000 more were added, and at Maynooth 35,000, including eight professors and 250 students. In 1843 he crossed to England, where, notwithstanding riots and other opposition, 600,000 signed during his short stay.

An amusing incident occurred one day at his own house in Cove Street at a dinner-party. One of the party, a most rigid abstainer, thought the flavour of the water was rather suspicious, and glanced at the servant, whose nose was more than usually red, while another could not refrain from tittering. At last Father Mathew put his glass to his lips, but at once replaced it on the table, saying, "John, what a strange taste and smell the water has ! What is the matter with it ? You must have had spirits in the jug." "Oh, yes, sir, I had to polish the tins, and whisky is very good for brightening them. Unfortunately, I put it into this jug." The younger guest inwardly chuckled at the excuse ; but Father Mathew only remarked that "it was all right," and that he would not trouble him for any further explanation.

He also used to say, "Now, there are some people, and sensible people too, who assert that plum puddings cannot be made without alcohol, but that is as fine a pudding as I ever tasted, and there is not of whisky in it, is there, John ?" "Oh, no sir ; not a drop," was the invariable reply.

It may be also interesting to notice some of the results which followed the extraordinary success which attended these labours. In the first place, it was found that just in proportion as the numbers of those who signed the pledge *increased*, the taxes upon malt and whisky *decreased.* From the time Father Mathew signed the pledge down to 1842, there was a total *loss* of £795,677, but there had been such an increased consumption of other exciseable articles, that not only was that amount made up, but there was a *gain* of £90,823. One who was competent to speak said : " The scale kicked the beam, not on the wrong but on the right side. The nation's books, though the whisky-traders dealt so little with her, were not the worse, but the better. Tea and sugar yielded an increase of 10 per cent. A draper in the poorest part of Dublin bore testimony that his trade had increased sixteen-fold since the whisky was abjured. Crime and violence were most sensibly lessened ; and on all hands, and on every side, the revenue was recouped for the absence of the blood-stained coins of the traffic. Incomings increased, outgoings decreased, two signs evident of well-doing, whether for the pocket of the citizen or for the coffers of the nation."

A Royal Commission also reported that "not a single teetotaler out of the millions was implicated in the guilt of blood-shedding ; the convicts were all whisky-drinkers." While those who were hanged for murders *before* the movement commenced numbered 66, in 1845 only 13 were so sentenced ; in 1839 there were 916 transported, in 1845 only 428 ; in 1839 there

were 12,049 committed to gaol, in 1845 only 7,101
The key to the whole mystery may be traced in
the following significant facts : In 1839 there were
12,296,000 gallons of whisky charged with duty to
the amount of £1,434,573, but in 1845 there was only
6,450,137, which realised a duty only of £860,151.

Referring, as matters often did, to such facts, he
once said :—" I do not know but that there are distillers or brewers listening to me.　I have such in my own
family.　One member of my family, in Cashel, a
distiller, now manufactures, I am glad to say, as
much in a week as would supply his customers for a
year.　That is a great falling off from other days..　I
am rejoiced at this ; for when the glory of God is in
question we should not mind the ties of flesh and
blood."　That it was serious to some of them may be
gathered from the following letter from a member of
the Mathew family, who wrote in 1843 : " Every
teetotaler has gained morally and physically by the
movement ; but my immediate family have been
absolutely and totally ruined, by Father Mathew's
Temperance Mission."

A gentleman was one day complaining of Father
Mathew's severity towards distillers, and saying that
they had so much money invested in the business
that it could hardly be expected they would give
it up ; to which Father Mathew said that such men
had no right to prosper by the ruin of others.　He
then told them that one day he was met by a very

rich distiller, who asked him, rather imploringly, how he could deliberately plot the ruin of so many un-offending people, who had their all invested in distil-leries? In reply, he said : "A very fat duck went out early one morning in pursuit of worms, and after being out all day, she succeeded in filling her crop, and on her return home at night, with her crop full of worms, she had the misfortune to be met by a fox, who at once proposed to take her life to satisfy his hunger. The old duck appealed, argued, implored, and remonstrated. She said to the fox, 'You cannot be so wicked and hard-hearted as to take the life of a harmless duck merely to satisfy your hunger.' She exhorted him against the commission of so great a sin, and begged him not to stain his soul with her innocent blood. When the fox could stand her cant no longer, he said, 'Out upon you, madam! with all your fine feathers, you are a pretty thing to lecture me about taking life to satisfy hunger. Is not your own crop now full of worms? You destroy more lives in one day to satisfy your hunger than I do in a whole month!'"

When his relative wrote to him, and said, "If you go on thus you will certainly ruin our fortune," his answer was, "Change your trade ; turn your premises into factories for flour. At all events, my course is fixed. Though heaven and earth should come together, we should do what is right." Such unselfish and dis-interested conduct is worthy of imitation at all times.

Like other earnest temperance reformers, Father Mathew by no means confined his efforts to this one thing. He was an earnest advocate of law and order, and protested with the most ardent manner against "secret societies"; and on several occasions he availed himself of the occurrence of some terrible outrage to give the people warnings. "My dear friends," he said, "I caution you not to join them [secret societies], whatever name they bear. If any of these emissaries address you, at once disclose the matter to your clergyman or to the next magistrate, for these bloodthirsty wretches only seek to betray you, and, having effected their object, they would then go to a foreign land, there to live on the blood-money." How wise and wholesome these counsels were, the events of the past few years abundantly confirm.

During his stay in London several amusing incidents occurred. We can only find space for two. At a large party Father Mathew tried to make a convert of Lord Brougham. "I drink very little wine," said Lord Brougham; "only half a glass at luncheon and two half glasses at dinner; and though my medical advisers told me I should increase the quantity, I refused to do so." "They are wrong, my lord, for advising you to increase the quantity, and you are wrong in taking the small quantity you do; but I have my hopes of you;" and after a pleasant resistance on the part of the noble lord, Father Mathew invested him with the ribbon and medal. "I will

keep them," said Lord Brougham, "and take them to
the House, where I shall be sure to meet with Lord——
the worse for liquor, and I will put them on him." He
did so, for on meeting with Lord ——, who was so
noted for his drinking habits, he said, " Lord ——, I
have a present from Father Mathew for you," as he
passed the ribbon quickly over his neck. " Then I
tell you what it is, Brougham: I will keep sober for
this night," a vow which he performed, as much to
the amazement as amusement of his friends.

On another occasion he met with the Duke
of Wellington, and ·while conversing with him,
said, " I ought to claim your Grace as one of ours."
" How can that be, Father Mathew? I am not a
teetotaler, though I am a very moderate man," replied
the duke. " Oh, but you are a temperance man, your
Grace ; for if you had not so cool a head, you would
not have been the illustrious Duke of Wellington,"
was the quick reply.

A poor woman one day asked Father Mathew to
intercede with the Duke of Wellington to get her son
released as a recruit, who had taken the " shilling "
while drunk. He had no money to buy the poor
fellow's discharge, but, acting on the impulse of his
own generous nature, he wrote an earnest appeal to
the " Great Duke," stating that the man was the only
support of his mother and six children. By return of
post, he had the joy of receiving the following short,
but satisfactory, answer :—" Field Marshal the Duke

of Wellington presents his compliments to the Very Rev. Mr. Mathew : he could not refuse his application, and has directed the discharge of the soldier he desired."

During one of his visits to Westminster, the *Times* newspaper tells us, that " after giving the pledge to the second batch, Father Mathew said that while he was below he had heard one person say to his neighbour, ' What a shame it was that a Protestant should receive a blessing from a Catholic priest.' Now, since he had been in England, he had everywhere received the blessings of the Protestants, and he was proud of it. If a blessing did them no good, surely it could do them no harm. Since he had been in the country he had got half a million of blessings from the Protestants. He was daily saluted with ' God bless you, Father Mathew !' ' God speed you, Father Mathew !' and such-like earnest expressions. There certainly could be no evil in a blessing, come from where it would."

It was in this generous, large-hearted spirit that he everywhere carried on his work, and it would be well if we had more of it manifested by others in the world day by day.

In 1846 and 1847 Ireland was visited by a terrible famine, through the blight on the potatoes. Previously the country had on several occasions suffered in that way, but this was the most fatal of all. Father Mathew, while travelling to promote the spread of temperance, met with so many appalling facts, that he, with the promptness and humanity which ever marked his conduct, made a timely appeal to the Government for aid, in which ∙ he used the following startling words :—"Men, women, and children are gradually wasting away. They fill their stomachs with cabbage-leaves, turnip-tops, &c. &c., to appease their hunger. There are at this moment more than five thousand half-starved wretched beings begging in the streets of Cork. When utterly exhausted, they crawl to the workhouse to die." Death was everywhere, in the cabin, on the highway, in the cellar, and even in the streets. Over 2,000 died in the Cork Workhouse in four months. As many as sixty-seven were buried in one day. Into the work of helping and securing help Father Mathew threw all his energies, and spent his last shilling. Over £3,000,000 was spent in food, and according to the testimony of Sir John Burgoyne, it was "the grandest attempt ever made to grapple with famine over a whole country." It was accomplished through more than 2,000 committees. Yet with all this help, in nine months 10,000 persons had been buried in the cemetery at Cork alone. Father Mathew in this terrible crisis fully earned another title as "The Apostle of Charity."

The numerous calls upon his benevolence, together with the expenses connected with his temperance work, at length brought him financial difficulties of a very serious character. An effort was therefore

commenced, to assist him in such a way as to relieve
his mind from anxiety. In consequence of this, the
attention of her Majesty's Government was called to
the services Father Mathew had rendered to the
public peace and to the cause of humanity. The result
was, that her Majesty not only bestowed a pension of
£300 upon him, but also recognised that there are
other victories than those won in the field of battle
or on the quarter-deck, and that conquerors are to be
found among those whose hands are not crimsoned
with human blood. The good news was made known
to Father Mathew by Lord John Russell, whose letter
stated that it was given as a mark of her Majesty's
"approbation of your meritorious exertions in com-
bating the intemperance which in so many instances
obscured and rendered fruitless the virtues of your
countrymen." With the pension he was able to
insure his life for an amount sufficient to cover all
his liabilities.

It was in the year 1848 that he first began to
suffer the penalty of his ten years' marvellous
exertions. Time was when he could say, "I am the
strongest man in Ireland;" but during Lent, just as
he was rising at an early hour, he fell to the ground,
and on the physician asking what was the matter, he
replied, in a calm voice and with a sweet smile, "I am
paralysed on one side." It turned out to be too true.
During the following months he seemed to rally, and
in 1849 he resolved, in opposition to the remonstrance

of his physician and friends, to pay his long-standing engagement to visit America. After a tedious voyage he arrived in safety, and on the 2nd of July he received a hearty welcome from the people in New York. He remained two years at his work, notwithstanding occasional attacks of paralysis. On the 8th November, 1851, he gave his farewell address to the people of the United States, in which he stated he had visited twenty-five States of the Union, and given the pledge to 300 of the principal towns and cities, travelling 37,000 miles for the purpose. "Though," he adds, "the renewed attacks of a painful and insidious malady have rendered it impossible that I could (without imminent danger to my life) make those public exertions which were never spared by me in the days of my health and vigour, I yet, thank Heaven! have been instrumental in adding to the ranks of temperance over 600,000 disciples in America." He was then advised by his physician to take absolute repose, to which he gave the following noble reply :—"Never will I willingly sink into inglorious inactivity. My life cannot be sacrificed in a better cause. If I am to die, I will die in harness."

One day, towards the close of his life, Father Mathew was returning unusually animated from where he then lived to the city, when a lady remarked "Something must have pleased you very much ;" to which he replied, "I have been invited to dinner by the little son of a respectable working-man, who has met me in the street. 'Father Mathew,' said the little fellow, 'do come and dine with us; we have such a nice dinner.' 'What have you, my dear?' I asked. 'We have a fine leg of mutton, and we have turnips, and we have potatoes,' replied the child. 'Have you no cakes?' I asked. 'No, sir,' answered the child, feeling somewhat ashamed at having given me an invitation with such a deficiency. 'Then, my dear, you must have them,' said I, as, putting my hand in my pocket, I gave him half-a-crown to go and get them."

In one of his addresses he tells us that a corn dealer in Cork, named Barry, was one day met when on his way to the savings-bank by a whisky dealer, who said to him with an inquisitive look, "Why is it that you do not come to see me now, my friend, so often as you used to do?" To this the other replied, "I cannot do any such thing now; my friend, Father Mathew has desired me to keep from temptation." "I am sorry to see you looking so very badly; your face is quite yellow!" "Why," said Barry, "if my face is yellow, so is my pocket too;" and he pulled out four sovereigns, which he was going to pay into the bank.

Looking back, amid his sufferings, at the vastness of the work he had done, and the great results which had followed his labours, he saw very clearly that, in addition to his efforts which had been so successful in persuading the people to give up the use of intoxicating liquors as a beverage, something ought to be done to remove the temptation to drink out of their way, by stopping the manufacture and sale of such drinks. In a letter to the United Kingdom Alliance, dated Cork, February 21st, 1853, he thus gives his warmest adhesion to that Society :—" My labours, with the Divine aid, were attended with partial success. The efforts of individuals, however zealous, are not equal to the mighty task. The United Kingdom Alliance strikes at the very root of the evil. I trust in God the associated efforts of the many good and benevolent men will effectually crush *a monster gorged by human gore."*

Had he lived to see the marvellous results which have been accomplished by the closing of the public-houses on Sunday, not only in Scotland, but also in Ireland, he would have had his heart filled with joy and thankfulness, and felt assured that victory over the monster cannot be very long delayed from being declared, and the blessings of temperance fully and completely enjoyed by the people.

For four years he continued to suffer under the malady which preyed upon his vital strength, and at the close of the summer of 1856 he went to live at Queenstown, where he might often be seen loitering about. One day a friend called to see him, and found he was praying. Father Mathew rose from his knees, and the gentleman said, "Pardon me for disturbing your devotions," "My dear friend," he replied, "you

must join with me in my prayers to God; pray for
me." "For you, sir?" "Yes; I was praying that
God would prepare me for leaving this world, and
would forgive me for the sins I have committed."
Taking the visitor by the hand, he again asked him
to kneel with him. "What necessity is there for my
praying for you, Father Mathew?" "Oh! who can
be pure in the sight of God?" was the reply. "But
you have done so much good for mankind." "No,
no," said the humble man, in still more earnest tones,
"I have done nothing; and no one can be pure in
the eyes of God. Kneel with me, and pray with
me to the Father of mercy." They both knelt
and prayed, and arose from their knees radiant
with joy.

On December 2nd, 1856, he had a sixth stroke,
but lingered until the 8th, when, in the full enjoyment
of the powers of his mind, death stole upon him as
sleep upon a weary man, and thus he died in peace.
On the 12th his remains were deposited in the cemetery, and on October 10th, 1864, a monument was
erected to his memory in Cork, where it stands to the
memory of the great Apostle of Temperance, FATHER
MATHEW.

ELIHU BURRITT,

AMERICA'S LEARNED WORTHY.

———◆———

ELIHU BURRITT is a remarkable illustration of the power of taking care of "little things," "odd moments," and turning them to some practical account, instead of wasting them in dreams and idle wishes. Indeed, he makes no secret of the fact, that his first success in self-improvement is not to be set down to "genius," so called, but to the careful employment of those invaluable bits of time which so many waste. While he was working and earning his living as an ordinary blacksmith, he tells us that he managed to learn some eighteen ancient and modern languages, and twenty-two dialects. There is an abundance, also, of other facts which go to show that many persons have missed their way, not so much from want of ability, as from want of diligence in the right use of the proper means. Work is the price of success. Elihu Burritt recognised this to be the case, for he tells us that he found "hard labour *necessary* to enable him to study with effect;" and more than once he gave up school-teaching and study, and, taking to his leather apron again, went back to

E

his blacksmith's forge and anvil, for the sake of his health of body, as well as the welfare of his mind.

Elihu Burritt is also a striking proof in himself of the power of the people to rise—a grand illustration, we had almost said, of the compatibility of cheerful, willing, joyous toil with high, vast literary attainments. He was a working-man in the truest sense of the term. He could not have been an idler, or he would have died long before he did. He must work, either with his head or his hand ; and he presents a splendid reproof to those who are afraid to soil their hands or use their brains. He looked upon labour as something given to him by his Creator, and, like Himself, and it was for Him and to Him, when, either as the blacksmith or the philanthropist, he was toiling to lift himself and others into a better and higher life. He was a man of iron in the highest sense of the term, if by that we mean one possessed of solid, fixed principles, and bent upon conquering, and also possessing the stubbornness of iron, which can be so welded and refined, that it can be at last transformed into a bright and shining instrument for either ornament or use.

Elihu was the youngest of ten children. He was born on December 8th, 1810, in New Britain, Connecticut. Both his father and mother were noted for their piety and kindness to others, and although humble in circumstances, they brought up their children " in the fear and admonition of the Lord,"

Among the earliest recollections of Elihu's childhood, he tells us, was the arranging of all the chairs and stools in the house in a semicircle around the fire, and the benevolent expression of countenance with which his father used to conduct to the best seat in the family circle an old idiotic pauper, known by the name of " Aunt Sarah." Not that she held in reality such a relationship to the family, but it was the rule of that house, that if any one had met with the misfortune to lose a limb, or was halt, blind, or dumb, he became to their family an uncle, or, if a female, an aunt.

With such surroundings, it is easy to understand how it was that, after a hard day's work at the forge, in after days, Elihu was so ready to sit watching by his father's bedside while sick and dying, through half the silent hours of the night.

When about sixteen years of age, Elihu was apprenticed to a blacksmith, and began to live with his elder brother, Elijah, who, in consequence of his opposition to slavery, had been obliged to leave Georgia and return to his native town, where he had opened a school. It appears to have also been about that period that Elihu began first to manifest his diligence in the pursuit of knowledge. By the time he was one-and-twenty, when his term of apprenticeship was up, he laid aside the hammer, and became a student with his brother for six months. It does not appear that he had then any idea of the vastness of the work he was about to accomplish. He complied with his brother's wishes to study mathematics, Latin, and French, simply with the object of qualifying himself for a land surveyor, and being able to read a few works in their original tongue. But those winter's studies were the beginning of one of the most gigantic courses of mental and moral acquirements which the mind of man has ever triumphed over. He was then only able to earn a dollar and a half a day at his trade, and it might be considered that he spent that amount on schooling. This, however, only acted as an additional spur to his energy, and made him doubly industrious. By the expiration of the half-year he managed to acquire a good knowledge of mathematics, besides having read several French works, and gone through Virgil—no small task for so short a time.

He then resolved to go back to his forge, with the determination to make up for lost time. This he managed to accomplish by undertaking to do the work of two men; thus he also secured double wages. To do this he had to work fourteen hours a day; yet amid even these labours he still found time to proceed with his French and Latin studies in the morning and evening. He then also began to study Spanish and Greek, but he had to carry his Greek grammar in the crown of his hat, and make it his constant companion in the workshop. He frequently committed part of a Greek verb to memory while standing beside the furnace waiting for the metal to fuse. He spent about six months in this way, and then again left the forge, with the determination to employ his earnings in gaining more knowledge. To do this, during the winter he took lodgings at New Haven, where his intellectual labours and progress seem to have been perfectly marvellous. To use his own words :—" As soon as the man who attended the fires had made one in the sitting-room, which was about half-past four in the morning, I arose and studied German till breakfast, which was served at half-past seven. When the boarders were gone to their places of business, I sat down to Homer's ' Iliad,' without a comment to assist me, and with a Greek and Latin Lexicon. A few minutes before they came in to their dinners, I put away all my Greek and Latin, and began reading Italian, which was less cal-culated to attract the notice of the noisy men who at that hour thronged the room. After dinner I took a short walk, and then again sat down to Homer's ' Iliad,' with a determination to master it without a master. The proudest moment of my life was when I first possessed myself of the full meaning of the first fifteen lines of that noble work. *I took a tri-umphal walk in celebration of that exploit.* In the evening I read in the Spanish language until bedtime. I followed this course for two or three months, at the end of which time I read about the whole of the ' Iliad ' in Greek, and made considerable progress in French, Italian, German, and Spanish."

At the close of the winter he returned to his

native town, and once more put on his leathern apron, with a fresh determination to make up for lost time by diligence at the anvil. But by this time the fame of his learning had been noised abroad ; the result was, that he had an invitation to take charge of a grammar-school in a neighbouring town. This he accepted, and for twelve months not only attended most industriously to the pupils entrusted to his charge, but vigorously pursued his own studies. This, however, together with the want of the bodily exercise to which he had been accustomed, told upon his health to such an extent, that he relinquished his appointment at the school, and returned again to the forge.

Still, he did not give up his idea of searching for knowledge and acquiring information, but kept pushing away from time to time in fresh directions. By-and-by his mind was directed to the Oriental dialects, and to these he gave his attention ; but here a grave obstacle stared him in the face—the difficulty of obtaining the necessary books. Undaunted by this, he conceived the idea of working his passage across the Atlantic, in one of the ships to Europe, in order to get them. He started on his long journey, and actually walked to Boston, a journey of one hundred and twenty miles. Hearing on the road of the existence of an antiquarian library at Worcester, he turned his feet in that direction. While on his way, he was over-taken by a waggon, and succeeded in persuading the young driver to give him a friendly lift. While thus resting, he began to ponder how he could recompense his friend for the help received. To part with his little stock of money was impossible, as all he had was only a dollar. The only thing left was to tender his old watch in payment, and to tell the lad that if he could afford to have it repaired, it would be worth more than the cost of the ride, and hence, if the two should ever meet again, the " balance might be handed over to the original owner of the watch." These terms were agreed upon, and each went his way. Elihu obtained a situation as a journeyman blacksmith at Worcester, at twelve dollars per month, with board included. Some time after, he was surprised by a visit from the young waggoner, who came to him at the anvil, and smilingly handed him a few dollars, saying, at the same time, that the watch had been mended, and gave every satisfaction as a timekeeper. Time rolled on, and years passed away, when one day, while Burritt was travelling by railway from Worcester to his native town, New Britain, a well-dressed fellow-traveller accosted him, saying, " You have forgotten me, Mr. Burritt, but I have not forgotten you." Burritt acknowledged he had, and asked for further information. " You remember," said the traveller, " the boy to whom you gave your watch ? I am he : a young man, a student of Havard College." It may be readily conceived, that this led to a pleasant and hearty shaking of the hands, and then Burritt asked, " And about that watch ; what has become of

it ? for, to tell you the truth, I was much attached to
it, and should like to have it back again." "Then
you shall," replied the young man ; "you *shall* have it
back. I sold it ; but I know where it is, and it shall
be yours." In due time the watch was again in
Burritt's hands, and was retained by him, as one of
the greatest treasures he possessed, to the day of
his death.

During the time he resided at Worcester, with the
intention of availing himself of the privileges for study
which the antiquarian library gave him, he met with
another difficulty which developed his energy. It
arose in this way. The limitation of the hours during
which the library was open to the public proved a
barrier to his plans, and also a source of grief to
his mind. The library was only open to the public
at certain hours in the day, and these were the very
hours when he had to be at work, and confined to his
anvil. He continued, therefore, his Hebrew studies
unassisted, as he was best able. Every odd moment
he could steal out of the twenty-four hours was
devoted to study. He rose early in the winter
mornings, and while the mistress of the house was
preparing breakfast by lamp-light, he would stand
by the mantel-shelf, with his Hebrew Bible on the
shelf, and his Lexicon in his hand, thus studying as he
ate his breakfast. He did the same at his other meals.
It was in this way that he turned to good account
the other odd moments which his strong craving for

knowledge led him to deduct from his meal and other times. An extract or two from his own diary will give a better idea than anything else of the kind of life he was at that time leading :—

Monday, June 18th : Headache ; forty pages of Cuvier's "Theory of the Earth," sixty-four pages French, eleven hours' forging. *Tuesday :* Sixty-five lines of Hebrew, thirty pages of French, ten pages Cuvier's "Theory," eight lines Syriac, ten ditto Danish, ten ditto Bohemian, nine ditto Polish, fifteen names of stars, ten hours' forging. *Wednesday :* Twenty-five lines He-brew, fifty pages of astronomy, seven hours' forging. *Thursday :* Fifty-five lines Hebrew, eight Syriac, eleven hours' forging. *Friday :* Unwell ; twelve hours' forging. *Saturday :* Unwell ; fifty pages of Natural History, ten hours' forging. *Sunday :* Lessons for Bible Class.

It is not surprising to find that this constant strain upon the body and mind at last made great inroads upon his health. Yet he trudged along undaunted, merely saying, when suffering from headache, " A little less study and a little more work, say two or three hours' additional forging." In this way, as the years rolled by, he mastered, one after another, the Turkish, Ethiopic, and Persian languages, besides translating many of the Icelandic sagas for leading reviews, and also, on frequent occasions, delivering lectures on many topics. Generous offers were made by friends to ensure him rest from his manual work, so as to enable him to give more time to the cultivation of his mind ; but these, with the manly and true independence of his nature, he thankfully declined, and declared that "*the condition of journey-men or apprentices is the most advantageous for the acquisition of knowledge.*" Surely he was able to speak so from his own abundant experience.

No doubt every one who has heard of the "Learned Blacksmith" will be anxious to hear his own story, "Why I Left the Anvil!" He tells us: "One day I was tuning my anvil beneath a hot iron, and busy with the thought that there was as much intellectual philosophy in my hammer as in any of the enginery agoing in modern times, when a most unearthly screaming pierced my ears; I stepped to the door, and there it was, the great iron horse! Yes, he had come, looking for all the world like the dragon we read of in Scripture, harnessed to half a living world, and just landed on the earth, where he stood braying in surprise and indignation at the ' base use ' to which he had been turned. I saw the gigantic hexiped move, with a power that made the earth tremble for miles. I saw the army of human beings gliding with the velocity of the wind over the iron track, and droves of cattle travelling at the rate of twenty miles an hour, towards their city slaughter-house. It was wonderful. The little busy-bee-winged machinery of the cotton factory dwindled into insignificance before it. Monstrous beast of passage and burden! It devoured the intervening distance, and welded the cities together! But for its furnace heart and iron sinews, it was nothing but a beast, an enormous aggregation of—horse-power. And I went back to the forge with unimpaired reverence for the intellectual philosophy of my hammer.

"Passing along the street one afternoon, I heard a noise in an old building, as of some one puffing a pair of bellows. So, with no more ado, I stepped in, and there, in a corner of a room, I saw the *chef d'œuvre* of all the machinery that has ever been invented since the birth of Tubal Cain. In its construction it was simple and unassuming as a cheesepress. It went with a lever—with a lever longer, stronger, than that with which Archimedes promised to lift the world. 'It is a printing press,' said a boy standing by the ink-trough, with a queueless turban of brown paper on his head. 'A printing press? What do you print?' I asked. 'Print?' said the boy, staring at me doubtfully, 'why, we print thoughts.' 'Print thoughts?' I slowly repeated after him; and we stood looking for a moment at each other in mutual admiration, he in the absence of an idea, and I in pursuit of one. But I looked at him the hardest, and he left an ink mark on his forehead, from a pathetic motion of his left hand to quicken his apprehension of my meaning. 'Why, yes,' he reiterated, in a tone of forced confidence, as if passing an idea, which, though having been current a hundred years, might still be counterfeit for all he could show on the spot; 'we print thoughts, to be sure.' 'But, my boy,' I asked, in honest soberness, 'what are thoughts? and

how can you get hold of them to print?' 'Thoughts
are what come out of people's minds,' he replied.
'Get hold of them, indeed ; why, minds arn't nothing
you can get hold of, nor thoughts either. All the
minds that ever thought, and all the thoughts that
minds ever made, wouldn't make a ball as big as
your fist. Minds, they say, are just like air : you
can't see them ; they don't make any noise, nor
have any colour ; they don't weigh anything. Bill
Deepcut, the sexton, says that a man weighs just
as much when his mind has gone out of him as he
did before. No, sir, all the minds that ever lived
wouldn't weigh an ounce troy.' 'Then, how do you
print thoughts?' I asked. ' If minds are thin as air,
and thoughts thinner still, and make no noise, and
have no substance, shade, or colour, and are like
the winds and more than the winds, are anywhere
in a moment, sometimes in heaven, and sometimes
on earth, and in the waters under the earth, how
can you get hold of them ? how can you see them
when caught, or show them to others ? '

    "Ezekiel's eye grew luminous with a new idea,
and pushing his ink-roller proudly across the metallic
page of the newspaper, he replied, ' Thoughts work
and walk in things what make tracks ; and we take
them tracks and stamp them on paper, or iron,
wood, stone, or what not. That is the way we print
thoughts. Don't you understand ?' The pressman
let go the lever and looked interrogatively at Ezekiel,

beginning at the patch in his stringless brogans, and following up with his eye to the top of the boy's brown paper buff cap. Ezekiel comprehended the felicity of his illustration, and, wiping his hands on his torn apron, gradually assumed an attitude of earnest exposition. I gave him an encouraging wink, and so he went on. 'Thoughts make tracks,' he continued impressively, as if evolving a new phase of the idea by repeating it slowly. Seeing we assented to this proposition inquiringly, he stepped to the type-case, with his eye fixed admonishingly upon us. 'Thoughts make tracks,' he repeated, arranging in his left hand a score or two of metal slips, 'and with these here letters, we can take the exact impression of every thought that ever went out of the heart of a human man ; and we can print it too,' giving the inked forme a blow of triumph with his fist ; 'we can print it too, give us paper and ink enough, till the great round earth is blanketed around with a coverlid of thoughts as much like the pattern as two peas.' Ezekiel seemed to grow an inch at every word, and the brawny pressman looked first at him, and then at the press, with evident astonishment.

"'Talk about the mind's living for ever!' exclaimed the boy, pointing patronisingly at the ground, as if mind were lying there, incapable of immortality until the printer reached a helping hand ; 'why, the world is brimful of live, bright, industrious thoughts, which would have been dead, as dead as stone, if it hadn't been for boys like me who have run the ink-rollers. Immortality, indeed ! why, people's minds,' continued he, with his imagination climbing into the profanely sublime, 'people's minds wouldn't be immortal if 'twasn't for the printers—at any rate, in this here planetary burying-ground. We are the chaps what manufacture immortality for the dead men,' he subjoined, slapping the pressman graciously on the shoulder. The latter took it as if dubbed a Knight of the Legion of Honour, for the boy had put the mysteries of his profession in sublime apocalypse. 'Give us one good healthy mind,' resumed Ezekiel, 'to think for us, and we will furnish a dozen worlds as big as this with thoughts to order. Give us such a man, and we will insure his life; we will keep him alive for ever among the honey. He can't die, no way you can fix it, when once we have touched him with these here bits of inky pewter. He shan't die nor sleep. We will keep his mind at work, or all the minds that live on the earth, and all the minds that shall come to live here as long as the world stands.'

"'Ezekiel,' I asked, in a subdued tone of reverence, 'will you print my thoughts too ? '

"'Yes, that I will,' he replied, 'if you will think some of the right kind.' 'Yes, that we will,' echoed the pressman. And I went home and thought, and Ezekiel has printed my 'thought-tracks' ever since."

The circumstances under which he one morning found himself famous are worth special record. I had come to the knowledge of Mr. Everett, then Governor of Massachusetts, when Elihu was about twenty-seven years of age, that he could read *fifty* languages, many of which he had also mastered. At an association of mechanics Mr. Everett mentioned this in an address. When the tidings came to Burritt, he wrote : " I find myself involved in a species of notoriety not at all in consonance with my feelings. Those who have been acquainted with my character from my youth up will give me credit for sincerity when I say that it never entered my heart to blazon forth any acquisition of my own. I had, until the unfortunate denouement which I have mentioned, pursued the even tenour of my way unnoticed, even among my brethren and kindred. None of them ever thought I had any particular genius, as it is called. I never thought so myself." What a contrast this, to the panting after fame by those who never deserve it ! Again, in referring to the same subject, Burritt let us into the secret, if we may so call it, of his success. These are the words in which he makes it known : " All that I have accomplished, or expect or hope to accomplish, has been and will be by that plodding, patient, persevering process of accretion which builds the ant-heap, particle by particle, thought by thought, fact by fact. And if ever I was actuated by ambition, its highest and warmest aspiration reached no farther than the hope to set before the young men of my country an example in employing those invaluable fragments of time called 'odd moments.' And, sir, I should esteem it an honour of costlier water than the tiara encircling a monarch's brow, if my future activity and attainments should encourage American working men to be proud and jealous of the credentials which God has given them to every eminence and immunity in the empire of mind. These are the views and sentiments with which I have sat down night by night for years, with blistered hands and brightening hope, to studies which I hoped might be serviceable to that class of the community to which I am proud to belong. This is my ambition. This is the goal of my aspirations." This will be clearly seen if we also notice what he said on another occasion, when referring to his early career : " For the first five years of my residence in Worcester I devoted all the leisure hours which occurred in the intervals of manual labour to the study of languages, and to other literary pursuits, rather as a source of enjoyment than as the means of future usefulness. When my tastes for these recreations had strengthened almost to a passion, my mind was biased in a new direction by an incident which impressed it with the conviction that there was something to live for besides the gratification of a mere curiosity to learn : that there were words to be spoken with the living tongue and earnest heart, for great principles of truth and righteousness, as well as to be committed to a silent memory, from the dead languages of the ancient world. To that conviction I yielded the literary pre-dilections and pursuits which had engrossed my hours of leisure, and nearly all the thoughts I could divert from my daily avocation."

In 1844 he commenced the publication of a weekly newspaper, the *Christian Citizen*. It was specially devoted to anti-slavery, peace, temperance, and self-cultivation. In 1846 he visited England. During a three years' residence he originated enterprises, some of which were for promoting peace. "The League of Universal Brotherhood" at one time consisted of ten thousand members in Great Britain, and as many in the United States. Out of this sprang "The Olive-leaf Mission," its object being the insertion in about forty continental journals of articles on peace. In favour of ocean penny postage, he addressed 150 meetings in the United Kingdom, and travelled over nearly the whole of the United States on the same mission. In 1854 he began a six years' labour to get the people of America to adopt "compensated emancipation" as the safest, cheapest, and most equitable way of extinguishing slavery; but the descent of Old John Brown on Virginia led to a war which cost ten times more in money alone than if it had been done in the manner he proposed.

In 1858 he delivered a lecture to the Agricultural Society of New York, during which he thus referred to his early efforts in farming :—" I recollect I am

F

merely serving the third year of my apprenticeship in
agricultural life, and that all the farm I own is a small
sterile hill in Connecticut, so poverty-stricken and
exhausted when I acquired possession of it, that
only a few sickly daisies and jaundiced weeds showed
their diminished heads above the stones, which in
many places covered the ground three feet deep."
The idea of facing well-to-do large farmers was
therefore rather serious to him. Nevertheless, he
tells them how he stood up against their scoffs and
jeers, and that he had only one answer, and it was
this: "I wish to go into co-partnership with Divine
Providence in the work of creation; and if, by
virtue of that co-partnership, I could make two spires
of grass grow where one did not before, it was a work
as near a work of creation as man could attain to.
To the man who could grow corn, rye, and potatoes
on rich meadow land there was no merit, for Nature
would carry off seventy-five per cent. of the credit."

It was in the year 1837 he signed the temperance
pledge, and from 1840 to 1844 he lectured exten-
sively on the subject in America. He was one of
the most noted of the visitors who attended "The
World's Temperance Convention," held in London,
August, 1846. Among other contributions which
have proceeded from his pen are "The Drunkard's
Wife" and "Lead us Not into Temptation." He
was an ardent friend of the Juvenile Temperance
movement. His views were very decided and clear,

as may be gathered from his own life motto, which can be safely recommended to all even at this time. It was in these words :—

TOUCH NOT!
TASTE NOT!
HANDLE NOT!
SMELL NOT!
ANY THING THAT CAN INTOXICATE!

He had a favourite argument to show that the influence of the drunkard is all on the side of total abstinence, and that the greatest instrument pleading the cause, " with all the eloquence of his misery," is the drunkard ; and then he asks, " When the biting scoffs of men and dogs have chased him into his frosty retreat, and he stands at bay upon the straw on which a broken-hearted creature which he once called his wife is trying to die—what does he preach there ? Is it temperate, moderate drinking or total abstinence that he advocates, when his little shoeless, shivering children lift their cold feet out of the cold ashes, and, with faces stereotyped with haggard misery, fix on him their large, glassy eyes for bread ? "

Again he remarks :—

" The most brilliant genius and talents are no protection or safeguard against the fascinating and fettering power of strong drink. In every age, and in every country, learned, eloquent, and high-born men have fallen before this insidious tempter, and destroyer of the human race. These high qualities, so much admired and coveted by all classes of the community, do not rescue the victims of this foe, when once entangled in the meshes of its fascination. The height from which the gifted fall when they sink into the lowest depths of intemperance measures their misery to the eye of the spectator. We see in their fate the magnitude of the ruin which may be wrought by strong drink. We see how the strongest men are made weak before the intoxicating cup. Before this great enemy of man, as before the King of Terrors, the learned and illiterate, the artisan and statesman, the rich and poor, seem to be on an equal footing. There is no safety for either in a moment's dalliance with the tempter. Keep him at a distance. It is dangerous even to 'look upon the wine when it is red, and when it giveth its colour in the cup.'"

Once more, in speaking to farmers and others, he says :—"Drink, is it? Juleps, nectarine punches, and other artistic mixtures to delight the taste. Look into that dark, deep well, with the cold water just perceptible. This is a more delicious drink to the farmer than was ever distilled from nectar for Jupiter. He wants no golden or silver goblet to drink it from. The old oaken bucket, swinging on its iron swivel, is better to him than all the chased ware of luxury. See him at the windlass or well-sweep, with his face red and dusty, and his mouth, eyes, and throat chafed with hay-seed. Hear the big-bottomed bucket bump against the moss-covered stones as it descends. There is the splash, and the cold gurgling sound at the filling ; and now it slowly ascends, with a spray of water-drops dashing against the wall, every one giving a new edge to the farmer's thirst. There it is, standing on the curb before him, and it mirrors the moistened and reddened face which bends to the draught. There is a drink for you that Nature has distilled for the farmer's lips, the like of which fabled Olympus never knew."

He walked all over England, from Land's End to John o' Groats, in the spring and summer months, calling upon those who were noted for rearing horses, pigs, cows, and other animals. He made also calls upon growers of flowers, corn, and other produce, noting the special improvements and changes they had introduced in cultivation, or of alteration in their character.

During one of these journeys he says :—" I once heard it stated that a certain bombshell of a new pattern cost £11 when ready for use. Then it would cost the labour of an able-bodied man at the plough, sickle, and hoe for six spring and summer months, to pay for one of these death-dealing shells ! How much honest, patient labour is swallowed up in the wolfish maw of war ! "

One of his plans was to travel on foot, and meet the labouring classes in small rooms in the villages through which he passed. After spending two or three weeks in Manchester and Birmingham, he buckled on his knapsack and started. He walked one hundred and fifty miles in that way, holding such meetings at night. Often he had to arrange for larger meetings, such was the desire to hear him. A year thus rolled by, and wider doors of usefulness were opened to him ; and he then went on the Continent of Europe to disseminate the principles of peace. Ultimately he arranged for one of the most important conferences on the subject ever held. Distinguished men of different countries came to Brussels in 1848. This led to another meeting of the same character at Paris, and then in Germany and other places. Thus, step by step, he found his labours crowned with a success which at first he never contemplated or imagined.

Like other notable workers for the good of their fellows, Elihu Burritt availed himself of any opportunity which came within his reach to manifest his practical sympathy, irrespective of creed, party, or nation. One of the most notable of these occurred, when on a visit to Ireland in 1847, during the terrible famine. He was so much moved by the scenes he witnessed, that he penned an appeal to his fellow-countrymen for help, which he had the joy of knowing met with a very hearty response from the American nation.

Referring to this in one of his interesting books, he said :—" The very slaves of the South, at their rude cabin meals at night, thought and spoke of the hungry people somewhere beyond the sea, they knew not in what direction ; and they came with their small gifts in their hands, and laid them among the general contributions, each with a heart full of kindly feeling towards the suffering. Never was there such a rummaging in cellars, garrets, wardrobes, and granaries in the United States, for things that would be comfortable to the hungry and needy. Little children, in their small way of thinking, brought their cherry-faced dolls, with the idea that these would speak comfort out of their bead eyes to the starving babies in Ireland. The barrels and bags of flour, wheat, and Indian corn, the butter, cheese, and bacon, sent from the prairie farmers of the Western States, were marvellous for number and heartiness of contribution. From a thousand pulpits a thousand congregations of different creeds were invited to lend a hand to the general charity in a few earnest and feeling words about the Fatherhood of God, and the Universal Brotherhood of Men. The National Government were touched by the same impulse, and ordered out of their berths two great war-ships, to convey a portion of the people's offerings to Ireland. It was a pleasant sight to see those grim old frigates lay off their armour, and put on the most peaceful civilian dress that any ships ever wore abroad. One of them was a frigate captured from the British navy in the last war between the two countries. Its port-holes, now showing double rows of limbered flour-barrels, charged full to their heads and hoops with the best brands of wheat powder, once belched forth fire, smoke, and hissing bolts of destruction in the angry parlance of battle with its American opponent. Landseer's white lamb looking into a dove's nest, in the mouth of a half-buried cannon, does not make such a good picture of Peace as he might have made of those two frigates, washed and shaved, and walking with a good-natured sailor's roll across the ocean, with all their huge pockets full of bacon, bread, and cheese for the hungry Irish."

From his " Sparks from the Anvil " we cull what is considered his finest production. It is entitled, " The Natural Bridge ; or, One Inch the Highest." The scene opens with a view of the great Natural Bridge in Virginia. There are three or four lads standing in the channel below, looking up with awe to that vast arch of unhewn rocks which the Almighty bridged over those everlasting butments, " when the morning stars sang together." The little piece of sky spanning these measureless piers is full of stars, although it is midday. It is almost five hundred feet from where they stand, up those perpendicular bulwarks of limestone, to the key-rock of that vast arch, which appears to them only of the size of a man's hand. The silence of death is rendered more impressive by the little stream that falls from rock to rock down the channel. The sun is darkened, and the boys have unconsciously uncovered their heads, as if standing in the presence-chamber of the Majesty of the whole earth. At last this feeling begins to wear away; they look around them; they find that others have been there before them. They see the names of hundreds cut in the limestone butments. A new feeling comes over their young hearts, and their knives are in their hands in an instant. "What man has done man can do," is their watchword while they draw themselves up, and carve their names a foot above those of a hundred full-grown men who have been there before them.

They are all satisfied with this feat of physical exertion except *one*, whose example illustrates perfectly the forgotten truth that there is *no royal road to intellectual eminence.* This ambitious youth sees a name just above his reach—a name that will be green in the memory of the world when those of Alexander, Cæsar, and Bonaparte shall sink into oblivion. It was the name of Washington. Before he marched with Braddock to that fatal field, *he* had been there, and left his name a foot above all his predecessors. It was a glorious thought of the boy to write his name side by side with that of the great "father of his country." He grasps his knife with a firmer hand, and, clinging to a little jutting crag, he cuts a notch into the limestone, about a foot above where he stands; he then reaches up and cuts another for his hands. 'Tis a dangerous adventure; but as he puts his feet and hands into those notches, and draws himself up carefully to his full length, he finds himself a foot above every name chronicled in that mighty wall. While his companions are regarding him with concern and admiration, he cuts his name in rude capitals, large and deep, into that flinty album. His knife is still in his hand, and strength in his sinews, and a new-created aspiration in his heart. Again he cuts another niche, and again he carves his name in larger capitals. This is not enough. Heedless of the entreaties of his companions, he cuts and climbs again. The graduations of his ascending scale grow wider apart. He measures his length at every notch he cuts. The voices of his friends wax weaker and weaker, till their words are finally lost on his ear. He now, for the first time, casts a look beneath him. Had that glance lasted a moment, that moment would have been his last. He clings with a marvellous shudder to his little niche in the rock. An awful abyss awaits his almost certain fall. He is faint with severe exertion, and trembling from the sudden view of the dreadful destruction to which he is exposed. His knife is worn half-way to the haft. He can hear the voices, but not the words, of his terror-stricken companions below. What a moment! What a meagre chance to escape destruction! There is no retracing his steps. It is impossible to put his hands into the same niche with his feet, and retain his slender hold a moment. His companions instantly perceive this new and fearful dilemma, and await his fall with emotions that " freeze their young blood." He is too high, too faint, to ask for his father and mother, his brothers and sisters, to come and witness or avert his destruction. But one of his companions anticipates his desire. Swift as the wind he bounds down the channel, and the situation of the fated boy is told upon his father's hearthstone.

Minutes of almost eternal length roll on, and there are hundreds standing in that rocky channel, and hundreds on the bridge above, all holding their breath and awaiting the fearful catastrophe. The poor boy hears the hum of new and numerous voices both above and below. He can just distinguish the tones of his father, who is shouting with all the energy of despair: " *William! William! Don't look down; your mother, and Henry, and Harriet are all here, praying for you! Don't look down; keep your eye towards the top!* " The boy didn't look *down*. His eye is fixed like a flint towards heaven, and his young heart on Him who reigns there. He grasps again his knife. He cuts another niche, and another foot is added to the hundreds that remove him from the reach of human help below. How carefully he uses his wasting blade! How anxiously he selects the softest places in that vast pier! How he avoids every flinty grain! How he economises his physical powers, resting a moment at each notch he cuts! How every motion is watched from below! There stand his father, mother, brother, sister, on the very spot where, if he falls, he will not fall alone.

The sun is now half-way down the west. The lad has made fifty additional niches in that mighty wall, and now finds himself directly under the middle of that vast arch of rocks, earth, and trees. He must cut his way in a new direction to get from under this overhanging mountain. The inspiration of hope is dying in his bosom; its vital heat is fed by the increasing shouts of hundreds perched upon cliffs and trees, and others who stand with ropes in their hands on the bridge above, or with ladders below. Fifty notches more must be cut before the longest rope can reach him. His wasting blade strikes again into the limestone. The boy is emerging painfully, foot by foot, from under that lofty arch. Spliced ropes are ready in the hands of those who are leaning over the outer edge of the bridge. Two minutes more, and all will be over. The blade is worn to the last half-inch. The boy's head reels; his eyes are starting from their sockets. His last hope is dying in his heart; his life must hang upon the next notch he cuts. That niche is his last. At the last faint gash he makes, his knife—his faithful knife—falls from his little nerveless hand, and, ringing along the precipice, falls at his mother's feet. An involuntary groan of despair runs like a death-knell through the channel below, and all is still as the grave. At the height of nearly three hundred feet the devoted boy lifts his hopeless heart and closing eyes to commend his soul to God. 'Tis but a moment—there! One foot swings off! He is reeling—trembling—toppling over into eternity! Hark! A shout falls on his ears from above. The man who is lying with half his length over the bridge has caught a glimpse of the boy's head and shoulders. Quick as thought the noosed rope is within reach of the sinking youth. No one breathes. With a faint, convulsive effort, the swooning boy drops his arms into the noose. Darkness comes over him, and with the words " *God !* " and " *Mother !* " whispered on his lips just loud enough to be heard in heaven, the tightening rope lifts him out of his last shallow niche. Not a lip moves while he is dangling over that fearful abyss ; but when a sturdy Virginian reaches down and draws up the lad, and holds him up in his arms before the tearful, breathless multitude, such shouting—such leaping and weeping for joy—never greeted the ear of a human being so recovered from the yawning gulf of eternity.

A crowded meeting was held in the North Church, Boston, to give the " Learned Blacksmith," as they called him, a reception home in 1850, at which he gave the following summary of his experience :—" I went out from your midst a timid young man with the meekest aspirations and humblest hopes. I went away pensively on foot, carrying under my arm all I owned in the world tied up in a small handkerchief. So far as I can recall the thoughts which passed my mind during the long walks of that pedestrian journey, I can truly say that a life of contented and obscure usefulness was the height of my earthly ambition. My anticipations had this extent, and no more. And I can say with equal truth and sincerity, and I desire to say it gratefully, on this the most distinguished occasion that I have ever seen or ever expect to see in life, that if my course has diverged from that condition in which I had expected to pass my days, not unto me be the merit or honour of the change, but to that kind and over-ruling Providence which has led me, by a series of almost imperceptible stages, into a field of labour and experience of which I had no conception when I left New Britain in 1837."

After cherishing lofty purposes, performing deeds of kindness, and making untiring efforts such as had never been attempted by any one else before for the promotion of education, peace, temperance, and universal brotherhood among all with whom he had to do, he returned to his native town in 1870 to reside. There, when he had nearly reached the age of three-score years and ten, on the 8th of March, 1879, he passed away to his reward, leaving us to own that, of all who have given to the world a grand example of self-culture and self-sacrifice for the good of others, none have ever excelled the " Learned Blacksmith," who, although some may despise him, because of his lowly birth and plodding industry, has, notwithstanding, proved himself to be one of Nature's real noblemen, though he is only known as plain ELIHU BURRITT.

JOSEPH LIVESEY,

ENGLAND'S TEMPERANCE PIONEER.

—◦◦—

JUST at the beginning of this century, down in a damp cellar, there might have been seen two men and a boy working at three hand-looms, in which the elder had invested all the money he could spare to help his son's business. It could also have been easily perceived that they were struggling hard against difficulties, and that there seemed very little hope of either of them ever making for himself a name, which would be handed down to posterity with honour as having laid the foundation of the greatest and most successful social revolution of the times in which we live. Yet so it was. The youth who was sitting in that corner of yon damp cellar, with his back close to the wet wall, trying to combine reading and working together, was Joseph Livesey, the venerated founder of the Temperance Movement in England. The eldest of the three was his grandfather. The third, Thomas, was the youth's uncle.

Seven years or so before, on March 5th, 1794, Joseph had made his first appearance in the world, at a small cottage in Walton-le-dale, about one mile and a half from Preston. His father and mother were poor, hard-working people, but both delicate in health. A brother and sister had died early ; in 1801, both parents were carried off, within ten weeks of each other, by consumption. Thus, at the early age of seven, little Joseph was left without father, mother, sister, or brother, an orphan upon the wide world, with the natural questions, "What was to be done with him ? Where was he to go ? How was he to live ?" His grandparent, amid his own poverty, found him a home, and it is there we first meet with him.

With a feeble constitution to start with, and inheriting a tendency to consumption from both parents, it is the more surprising how he was able, from early morn till late at night, to endure such exposure and damp. But the fact that he did so illustrates very forcibly what strong common sense and a resolute will can accomplish, when united with perseverance and energy, and how possible it is to triumph over what at first sight appears to be an almost insurmountable barrier and to rise from a very humble origin, to occupy a place in the front rank among the "World's Workers."

He not only had the sorrow of losing both his parents, but his grandfather soon after his adoption had the misfortune to fail in the cotton business in which he had embarked his all. Mr. Livesey, speaking of this time, says : " I remember well the old man, on a Tuesday night, upon the return of Thomas (his son) with unfavourable reports from the Manchester market, crying like a child. Young as I was, I busied myself in the warehouse, sometimes at the warping mill, sometimes helping to hook pieces, or weighing out the weft. The 'moutre' trade was then carried on to a great extent, and the disputes with weavers and threats of 'bating' were frequent. Both yarn and cloth were enormously dear ; so there was a great temptation to weavers to sell cops, to take off 'half beers,' and by obliterating the 'smits' to get longer 'fents' than they were allowed." However, the crash came ; the only consolation left being that the assets realised enough to pay all the creditors twenty shillings in the pound.

The next step was back to a "weaving" farm where young Joseph had also to go with them. They were so poor that the lad had to act as a servant. "From necessity," he tells us, " I became pretty proficient in all kinds of labour connected with domestic life, and I have never regretted this ; for in speaking to the poor during my visitations, I have found my early experience of great service ; and in the event of any reverse, I have always felt I was prepared to live where others would perhaps starve."

Thus animated with a desire to make his way in the world, he kept pushing along. At the close of the day, when tired with toil on the loom, he thought

G

" there was something better ahead." This roused his
energies, and caused him to sit down bravely to a few
hours' more study.   Like David Livingstone, another
weaver boy, he resolved upon cultivating his mind, as
the best step to self advancement, and, like the
missionary, he learnt to work and read at the same
time.

There were no school boards in those days, so he
went for a short time to an old woman who kept a
dame's school.   There he learnt to read the Bible, and
then the cellar became his school-room, and the three
hand-looms at which his grandfather and uncle
worked. his desk.   Speaking of these times he says:
" This cellar was my college, the 'breast-beam' was
my desk, and I was my own tutor.   Many a day and
night have I laboured to understand Lindley Murray,
and at last, by indomitable perseverance, which long appeared a hopeless task, this was accomplished, without
aid from any human being.   Anxious for information,
and having no companions from whom I could learn
anything, I longed for books, but had no means with
which to procure them.   There was no public library,
and publications of all kinds were expensive ; and if
I could succeed in borrowing one, I would devour it
like a hungry man would his first meal."

Living, as we do, surrounded with schools, libraries,
and cheap literature, it is hard to realise the differ-
ence, so as to contrast it with the state of things
with which he had to contend.   Then he adds:

" At the period I refer to there were no national schools, no Sunday-schools, no mechanics' institutions, no penny publications, no cheap newspapers, no free libraries, no penny postage, no temperance societies, no tea parties, no Young Men's Christian Associations, no people's parks, no railways, no gas, no anything, in fact, that distinguishes the present time in favour of the improvement and enjoyment of the masses. Most of the articles of necessity for a poor man's house, during the war with France, were nearly double their present price, and all felt the pressure of the times. My only pocket money, when a lad, was ' the Sunday penny.' I have a distinct recollection how proud I felt when I went among my companions on the Sunday afternoon, with my threepence in my pocket, which was my increased weekly allowance. It was then I got my grammar, exercises, and key, Cann's Bible with references, and a few other books, as my means would allow. I seldom got a meal without a book open before me at the same time, and I managed to do what I have never seen any other weaver attempt, to read and weave at the same time. For hours I have done this, and without making bad work. The book was laid on the breast beam, with a cord slipped on to keep the leaves from rising ; head, hands, and feet all busy at the same time. I had a restless mind, panting for knowledge, and incapable of inaction. That part of the loom and the wall nearest my seat was covered with marks,

which 1 had made to assist me to remember certain
facts, and these hieroglyphics were there when I left.
This cellar is only a short walk from where I am now
writing, and I feel a pleasure in making a call at this
hallowed spot. The privations connected with
poverty, in my case, admitted of no exceptions. The
day seemed too short for my love of reading, and, as
often as I could, I remained to read after uncle and
grandfather had retired to bed ; but I was allowed no
candle, and for hours I have read by the glare of the
few embers left in the fire-grate, with my head close
to the bars. I had hard exercising ground, but still I
think it was well fitted, in a case like mine, to prepare
me for the battle of life I had to fight."

Referring again to this period in after years, he
had the honesty and manliness to say, " I once was
glad to pick up a stray leaf, or to borrow an old
backless book, with which to allay my thirst for
knowledge." Still the days were too short to satisfy
his thirst for knowledge. He was always anxious to
reach the end of a book, and when he once began to
read the first page, he did not care to lay it down
until he had reached the last. Contrasting the advantages which are within the reach of the young
people of the present day against those with which he
had to struggle, he says :—

" Whilst thousands of costly volumes lie dormant,
unopened, and unread by their owners, the backless
volume was read by me with eagerness, and this

doubtless has been the case with others. What would I not have given at that day to have had the opportunity afforded by the Preston Institution, a privilege too much undervalued by the working-classes of the present time. And yet it is a question in many cases, whether want or plenty makes the most sterling character. My first book-case consisted of two slips of wood, value about eightpence, hung to the wall by a cord at each end, and the first work placed upon these anti-aristocratic shelves was 'Jones's Theological Repository,' a periodical of a number of volumes which I had got at second-hand. I shall never forget, as I descended the cellar stairs, how I sometimes turned back to look at and admire my newly-acquired treasure."

It was this spirit of self-denial and self-reliance, embued with a deep sense of his great responsibility to a higher power, which ever marked his career, and gave such mighty impetus to his efforts. As an old writer more than two hundred and fifty years before had said : "Self-reliance and self-denial will teach a man to drink out of his own cistern, and eat his own sweet bread, and to learn and labour truly to get his own living, and carefully to save and expend the good things committed to his trust." These words express in the most graphic manner the ruling ideas which seem to have governed the life of Joseph Livesey. Village life seventy or eighty years ago was a very different thing to what it is now. The

contrast is most marked. The place where Joseph
Livesey lived was noted for its "fighting parties,"
and because he stoutly refused to join with them in
their brutal amusement, he had to stand the ordeal
of being taunted as "a softy." This, however, did not
hinder him from seeking his recreation in other directions. He says, for instance, that once he "followed
the hounds all day long in his clogs, but never desired
a repetition of that sport." Sometimes he went fish-
ing, and nothing gave him more delight than to stroll
by the silvery river Ribble, with some choice book
for a companion, and after laying night-lines below
Walton Bridge, to return home quite happy. It
will thus be seen that the less boisterous games were
more to his taste than the rough-and-ready sports
of the boys. Indeed, he confesses, "I generally made
the girls my companions, in preference to the boys."
He had no objection to a game at marbles, hide-and-
seek, forfeits, and joined heartily in the evening story-
telling parties, when "Jack the Giant-Killer," and
other like legends, formed the principal material
upon which their minds feasted. They believed in
"ghosts" and "bogies," and often amused themselves with repeating rumours of the exploits of a
local bogie called "Bannister Doll," until they became so excited that they had to be sent off to their
homes. Like every one else who looks around him,
Joseph, even in these days, could not help seeing how
the use of intoxicating drinks debases self-respect,

diminishes self-knowledge, defiles self-reverence, and destroys self-control ; hence it is not surprising to find that, on reviewing his life-long war against such drinks, on his eighty-first birthday, he asked, "Why should drink reign, and drink-selling tread national prosperity, domestic peace, morality, and religion under feet ?   Nothing, I believe, is wanting but a strong combined resolution, unity of action among all lovers of sobriety and goodness, and a willingness to sacrifice present and personal pleasure, for the deliverance and happiness of our fellow-creatures. Diffusive teetotalism and agitating teetotalism are what I long to see, and what I try to promote to the utmost of my present limited power."

As "example is better than precept," he could in fairness urge upon others to "go and do likewise," seeing that for over half a century he had, with an earnestness which never faltered, and a persistency which never flagged, as a true pioneer uttered his earnest convictions, and maintained his unswerving allegiance to the cause of temperance; and many a time when other subjects seemed for the moment to have absorbed the public mind, he successfully called back attention to the subject which lay nearest to his own heart, and so set an example of dogged, persistent determination not often manifested, and which has certainly never been surpassed.

It seems a wonder that, working for so many years close to the wet wall, that it did not produce immediate bad results, but he tells us why he thought it did not. "I can only suppose that this was counteracted in a great measure by the incessant action of almost every muscle of the body required in weaving. 'All fours' never cease action on the part of the hand-loom weaver. Yet it is very probable that the four rheumatic fevers that I have had to endure, and the seven years' chronic rheumatism in my lower joints, rendering me unable to walk about without pain, which followed, had their remote cause in that miserable place." Gradually he managed to improve, and get piece-work, and so to earn a little extra, with which he bought a grammar and a few other books. He also made several attempts to get lighter work. The shuttle-making was tried, without success; next "twisting-in" for weavers, then a jobber; this last employment failed so completely, that at the end of the week, by a trick of the trade, he did not receive a penny of wages.

One of the earliest recollections which stamped itself upon Joseph's mind was the procession of the famous Preston Guild in 1802. He was at that time eight years old, and the various products of cotton-spinning, which had only recently been introduced, formed a very marked feature in the day's proceedings. Preston at that time only contained a population of six or seven thousand inhabitants, but the manner in which the new industry was displayed made it very striking to his youthful mind. Referring to the display, the local historian tells us : "The gentlemen's procession commenced on Monday morning immediately after breakfast; it was preceded by the marshal, armed cap-à-pie, on horseback, etc. ; then came twenty-four young, blooming, handsome women, belonging to the different cotton-mills, dressed in a uniform of peculiar beauty and simplicity. The dress consisted wholly of the manufacture of the town. Their petticoats were of fine white calico ; the head-dress was a kind of blue-feathered wreath, formed very ingeniously of cotton, so as to look like a garland. Each girl carried in her hand the branch of an artificial cotton-tree as the symbol of her profession. The gentlemen walked in pairs, preceded by Lord Derby and the Hon. T. Erskine."

From that time onward Preston became a centre of bustling activity, until its population increased to upwards of one hundred thousand, and "King Cotton," as it has been called, converted the once aristocratic town of "proud Preston" into a beehive of industry, by which the people have been enabled to develop their energy, and secure for themselves a large addition to their comforts, of which in the early part of this century they had never dreamt.

When about sixteen years of age, he formed the acquaintance of a family residing in the village named Portlock. Such was the influence which their consistent Christian lives had upon him, that he resolved to accompany them to the Baptist chapel at Preston,

of which church they were members. Finally, it lead
to his being baptized, and joining the same church.
Speaking of the blessedness of this decision, and the
happiness it gave him, he. says, "The return of
Sunday was to me a feast of good things; all the
fervency of youth and zeal of a new convert were
added to a deep conviction of the importance of
religion. With what delight did I use to go, in my
clogs, to Preston to the evening prayer-meetings held
in the vestry. I have still in my possession Watts'
hymn-book, which I bought at the time. On the
inside of the front cover is written ' Joseph Livesey's
book, 1811.' On the blank leaf is the following : 'Is
any merry ? let him sing psalms' (James v. 13). And
at the end is the verse :

"Hope is my helmet, faith my shield,
 Thy Word, my God, the sword I wield ;
 With sacred truth my loins are girt,
 And holy zeal inspires my heart."

About that time he tramped, with fourteen others,
to Accrington, a distance of fourteen miles, to an
ordination service. He tells us: "The Rev. Mr.
Stephens preached from the text, 'One is your
master, even Christ ; and all ye are brethren.'
Equality was what I admired, and I was much
pleased with the discourse. At the close of the
service it was announced that any one who wished to
take dinner could be accommodated at a certain inn
at one shilling each. But I learnt that there was a

free dinner for the ministers and other rich friends. I felt, as one of the poor who really needed a dinner, and not having a shilling to spare, that the doctrine of equal brotherhood, though brilliant in the pulpit, was not so in 'word and deed.' But what offended me most was, that, being allowed to enter the large room after the dinner, I saw the minister and other friends enjoying themselves with their long pipes amid the fumes of tobacco, drinking spirits and other liquors. Though physically feeble, I was never deficient in moral courage, and when we were introduced to the reverend gentlemen, I could not forbear giving vent to my feelings. I protested against this eating and drinking, and said that in primitive times men were ordained to the ministry with 'prayer and fasting.' A poor, simple, ill-dressed, illiterate, unknown lad lecturing divines on the primitive duties of self-denial! A regular laugh was the response; and, indeed, what else could be expected? I believe this exhibition gave a cast to my mind of which I have never got clear, and I should be glad to believe that nothing similar is to be met with in the present day."

Over-confident of his own views, he tells us again that he "became the zealous advocate of opinions, rather than the promoter of charity among all good people," and this led him into a controversy in which he used this phrase, " I never see anything wrong but I am determined to set it right;" and although he met with a severe rebuke, it at the same time shows the resolute character of the young reformer when only about eighteen years old. He tells us that he " profited by the reproof, which he well deserved."

Not only had Joseph to contend with ignorance, but he had also to fight against vice. The moral world in which he lived was of the most poisonous character. Drunkenness was to be seen everywhere. The weavers believed in keeping what they called Saint Monday, and a queer kind of saint it was. The public-houses were crowded, and blasphemy and brutality could be seen and heard on every hand. Speaking of this he says : " We had a sad lot connected with the church. The grave-digger and his father were both drunkards. The ringers and singers were all hard drinkers ; and I remember the singers singing in my father's kitchen on a Christmas morning in a most disgraceful condition. The parish clerk was no exception. When the clock was standing on a morning for want of winding, as was often the case, the remark was, ' The clerk was drunk again last night.' I was surrounded by mental darkness and vice, and was without the companionship of congenial spirits."

It is said that " a dead dog can go with a stream, but it takes a living man to go against it." Hence it was needful for Joseph not only to resolve to lead a Christian life, but to do all he could to sustain its vigour and promote its efficiency. The result was, that soon after his conversion he resolved to become a Sunday-school teacher, then a prayer leader, and after that a preacher. His one desire was to elevate and save others.

He made up his mind to have a home of his own as soon as he could get one. At the age of twenty-one, by the death of a relative, he became possessed of the sum of £30. Meantime, he had heard of a Miss Williams, a religious girl, and with his usual earnestness, and before seeing her, he determined to make her an offer of marriage. Visiting the family with whom she was staying, he attended a prayer-meeting with them. He was asked to deliver an address, which he did. In after years Mrs. Livesey confessed it was owing to the favourable opinion she formed while he was speaking, more than anything else, that she was led to consent. He says, "We were fixed thirty miles from each other, and with the exception of about three visits, all the love-making, which lasted about a year, was done by long sheets of paper filled to every corner." Regardless of the jokes of friends, he attended auctions in the locality to buy articles of furniture cheap, so as to have the home ready when the wedding-day arrived, and on May 30th, 1815, at St. Peter's, Liverpool, "I remember," he says, "the parson gabbled over the service as quickly as possible, and I paid him a crown piece, remarking what a cheap wife I had got." She proved a real helpmate to him ; and for fifty years he could

say that his wife was the greatest blessing of his life
to him.   They went to their home at Walton, and he
says, "Here we both settled down to our work, Joseph
to his loom and Jane to her wheel; and though as
low in means as most people to start with, we have
'lived and loved together' now (1868) more than fifty-
two years, never once having reason to regret the
step we took.   I soon learnt the truth of the old
saying, 'In taking a wife you had better have a
fortune *in* her than *with* her.'"

Under his wife's excellent management the little
home became a palace.   In less than a year, however,
they had to remove into Preston, where Mrs. Livesey
gave birth to twins.   With bread, owing to the corn
laws, at a high price, wages low, and trade bad, it was
a gloomy outlook for Joseph; added to this, his
own health gave way.   He consulted the doctor,
and was ordered to live better, to take malt liquor,
and some bread and cheese in the middle of the
forenoon.   He bought a bit of common cheese at 7d.
or 8d. per lb.   That bit of cheese, however, proved to
be the pivot upon which his business career took a
turn.   The Lancashire cheese fair was being held,
and he happened to hear some one say that prices had
gone down to about fifty shillings the hundredweight.
By his self-taught arithmetic he discovered that
meant 5d. per lb.   He began to think if he could only
buy a whole cheese, and sell it out in small pieces to
his neighbours at that price, he could get a piece for

himself on the same terms. No idea of profit ever entered his mind. But where to get the money was the point. He ultimately thought of a draper named Burnett, who was known as a friend to those in need. He went and told his tale—how he could supply the poor with cheese at 5d. instead of 7d. In a minute the needful amount was lent, with which Joseph bought two cheeses at fourpence three-farthings a pound. He had then to go and borrow scales. After selling the cheese at fivepence halfpenny per pound, to cover the loss from cutting and weighing, he found he had made unintentionally a profit of 1s. 6d.; this was more than he could have earned in the same time by weaving. The news spread, and people kept coming for the cheap cheese ; so he gave up weaving, and took to cheese selling.

It was to this event that "weaving," so far as Joseph Livesey was concerned, came to an end. So he gave his loom to a poor man named Woodruff, thinking he had no further use for it; but by a strange coincidence he re-bought it back some years after for a sovereign, and had it made into a writing-table. Of this changed article of furniture he wrote in his seventy-fifth year : "Turn it over, and you will see the several pieces that constituted the cradle of my future usefulness ; and when I am in my grave, may this remind my children that their father was a poor man, and that of all the duties incumbent upon them they should never forget the poor."

It was no easy work to establish a business even in those days. Hence, we find that he had to attend the markets at Chorley, Blackburn, and Wigan, walking to and from Preston, railways then being a thing unknown. He then went to Bolton, and walked the double journey of forty miles and selling his cheese in one day. By degrees, with the help of friends lending him some money, he was able to buy a pony, which he had, however, to go and attend to himself. He then added a gig. By this means he was able to ride out into the country districts, and call upon the farmers and buy their cheese. During these journeys he met with many things to test his earnestness, and which also exposed him to serious risk and danger. On one occasion, when at Ulverston, owing to the heavy dew, he could not tell where he was, and wandered until he came to a farm-house, but even then he was afraid to knock, for fear they should take him for a bad character and set the dogs at him. So he sought an outhouse, and lay down on some hay until the morning, and then walked out without any one seeing him. On another journey, he was nearly overtaken by the tide whilst crossing the well-known Eleven-mile Sands, where so many have been drowned. He saw the waves rolling rapidly in from the west, and in an instant started eastward as fast as he could go, and managed in the narrowest way to escape. Once he was nearly in danger of being drowned, through the boatmen whom he had engaged to ferry him across the Wye being drunk. But nothing daunted his courage, or disheartened him in his purpose to succeed.

The claims of a family of thirteen children (four of whom died in infancy) acted as a spur to his energies. As the boys grew up they were put out to work, or made to take part in the business, and even before the parents became total abstainers no intoxicating drinks were kept in the house; water or milk was the usual drink.

In all these matters, and indeed in everything else, he was assisted by his wife ; and although when she knew he was writing his autobiography she said " See thou sayest nothing about *me*," it is pleasing to hear him own that " I cannot do justice to my feelings if I do not say a few words as to the excellencies of my dear wife. In our early struggles, when commencing business out of nothing, she was not only my counsellor in difficulties, but an active and efficient helper to the extent of, and even beyond, her power. She was no lady-wife ; though respectably connected, and accustomed to plenty before marriage, she willingly shared my poverty and privations, and bore a full part of our burdens. She shared my joys, and more than shared my sorrows, for she wiped them away. Whenever I was cast down, she was the one to revive my spirits. For a long time she did all the housework as well as attending to business, and she

H

would sit up past midnight making and mending the children's clothes. No pen could do justice in describing the sympathy she showed towards every sufferer that came within her reach ; nor set forth her willingness to undergo any toil to give them relief. If ever a 'good mother' existed, she deserves that name. . . . . . . A lady's life of soft indulgence, rising late in the morning, lolling on the sofa most of the forenoon reading novels, with little exercise, fed with rich food, and pampered with delicacies—these have killed many a thousand with better constitutions than Mother Livesey's."

Ten years at least before the Anti-Corn Law League began its work, Livesey, in one of his publications called *The Moral Reformer*, pleaded earnestly for free trade. He gave stirring facts showing that the average earnings of a man at weaving, working from five in the morning till ten at night, only amounted to 5s. 11¾d. per week, and then he added, " Such is the miserable pittance of the weaver. With provisions at the present exorbitant price, if any man can behold this state of things without raising his determined voice against it, he must be destitute of the common feelings of humanity."

Having learnt by painful experience, amid so many grave surroundings, the difficulty of obtaining an education himself, he set to work to help others around him, whom he discovered in the same condition. As there was no Sunday-school for adults, he opened his own cottage. His wife took the females, he took the males. When his house became too small for the scholars, he hired a large room and met them there.

A newspaper in those days cost sevenpence, and was therefore beyond the reach of working people, with such small wages as they then could earn. To meet this, on his own responsibility he opened his room for "a general reading-room," the charge being 3s. 3d. per quarter. Its success was so great, that he had to open six others in various parts of the town.

Early in life he felt the importance of the printing press, and began to use it, first with placards, then with pamphlets, and then with magazines. These were all issued amid the toil of his own business, and most of the articles were written by himself. This was no easy matter, when we consider that he had the cares of a large family, and the anxiety of creating and developing a business, on which they were dependent, and which for years mainly rested on himself. In addition to these, he issued a number of publications and tracts on various subjects, and while in 1844 he published the first number of the *Preston Guardian*, a newspaper which still exists, and stands among the foremost of the provincial papers of the country.

The circumstances under which Mr. Livesey took his "last glass" are so interesting that it is best to narrate it in his own words. In his annual Temperance address on New Year's Day, 1881, he says: "It is now fifty years since I took my last glass. It was early in 1831 at Mr. McKie's, Lime Street, Preston. It was only one glass of whisky and water. I often say it was the best I ever drank, the *best* because it was the *last;* and if I remain in my senses I shall never take another. I did not then understand the properties of alcoholic liquors, though I ought to have done, being thirty-seven years of age." The circumstances under which the event occurred ought to be named. A local manufacturer persuaded Mr. Livesey to join him in business as a sleeping partner, with the assurance that it was in a profitable and prosperous condition. Believing it to be so, Mr. Livesey invested all his spare cash. Soon after doing so, the trade began to fall off, creditors became pressing, and the manufacturer left the town, as well as the business, for Mr. Livesey to do as he might. To use his own words, "It was a trying time; after emancipating myself from the weaver's cellar, and labouring and toiling with my wife, almost night and day, with half-a-dozen children about our feet, to find, as we feared, all gone at once, by the treachery of one in whom we had confided as a friend, was a condition which experience alone will enable any one to realise. I was left to wind-up the business of which I was ignorant, and to provide for all its liabilities. At such a moment it is cheering to have a partner to share your burden, and keep up your spirits. 'Never mind,' said my dear wife, when she saw me cast down, 'we shall get through ; we worked hard for what we had ; it is lost, but we can work for more.' Time was given me ; I turned the stock into money, and by instalments paid every creditor the full amount of his claims. By this unhappy business I lost in money, time, etc., £2,000." The creditors, when the last instalment was paid, proposed to present him with a silver cup, as a mark of respect for his honourable conduct, but he declined it, saying "he had done nothing more than an honest man. ought to do." It was while thus engaged that Mr. Livesey had one day to meet some of his creditors in connection with this partnership, and a bottle of whisky was produced by the Scotsman as one of the usual methods of selling business in those days. "Either from its strength," says Mr. Livesey, "or from my never having taken whisky before, or more probably from a depression of mind I was labouring under at the time, it 'took hold of me.' I felt very queer as I went home, and retired to bed unwell. Next morning my mind was made up, and I solemnly vowed that I would never take any intoxicating liquors again, a vow which I have religiously kept to the present time. I had a large family of boys, and this resolution was come to, I believe, more on their account than from any knowledge I had of the injurious properties of the liquors."

He was not long ere he began to find the benefits

which resulted to himself, and on January 1st, 1832, the young men in his adult school by his advice formed a Temperance society, which at that time only meant abstinence from spirits and moderation in malt liquors. This was soon found to be a fatal snare, and led to serious disasters. One Thursday (August 23rd, 1832) John King was passing, and Joseph Livesey invited him in. " I asked him if he would sign a pledge of *total* abstinence, to which he consented. I then went to the desk and wrote one out. He came up to the desk, and I said, ' Thee sign first.' He did so, and I signed it after him." From these two signatures sprang the Total Abstinence movement in this country. A few days after, on Saturday, September 1st, 1832, a meeting was called in the Cock Pit, which had been built for cock-fighting, and would hold seven hundred persons. It was after moderation and total abstinence had been warmly discussed, that these seven men of Preston signed the following pledge:—"We agree to abstain from all liquors of an intoxicating quality, whether ale, porter, wine, or ardent spirits, except as medicines." At one of these meetings Richard Turner gave birth to the word *Teetotal* as denoting abstinence from *all* kinds of intoxicating drinks, and in the churchyard of St. Peter's Church there is a gravestone whereon the fact is recorded in these words : " Beneath this stone are deposited the remains of Richard Turner, author of the word ' Teetotal,' as applied to abstinence from all intoxicating liquors, who departed this life on the 27th day of October, 1846, aged 56 years."

It was about the year 1826 that a number of earnest philanthropists in America began to make an effort to organise themselves into an army, to check the onward march of the terrible vice of intemperance, with which they were being cursed. Gradually their labours were extended, and in 1829 the news reached England. From that time up to 1831 societies pledging their members to abstain from spiritous liquors gradually multiplied in number. But the honour of organising the *first* band of total abstainers from *all* intoxicating drinks must be claimed for the men of Preston. Here and there in many parts of the world, in all ages, there had existed men and women who had manifested by personal experience that all the duties of life could not only be discharged, but a great deal better discharged without intoxicating drinks; it was not, however, until by a combination of circumstances, which clearly indicated that God was directing the hearts and minds of some of His children to the matter, that anything in the shape of an organised effort was thought of, and it is nothing but right to own that the honour and credit of doing so ought to be ascribed to Joseph Livesey, who led the way.

From some years after Mr. Livesey signed the pledge, he devoted a large expenditure of time and money to platform work. He delivered in many parts of England and Scotland his "Malt Liquor Lecture," in which he demonstrated, by evidence which has never been refuted, that "there is more food in a pennyworth of bread than in a gallon of ale." To these efforts Dr. F. Lees, Thomas Whittaker, Jabez Inwards, and other well-known advocates, ascribe their first impressions, and subsequent labours, in support of the Temperance movement.

Wherever sorrow, suffering, and sin might be found, there Joseph Livesey was sure soon to direct his steps. His life was one constant effort to bless, elevate, and refine those who needed it. He believed in doing such a work himself, and never employed any deputy to relieve him, either of the work or its reward. Indeed, he watched over the cases as intently as if they were his own children. Forty years back he could therefore honestly say, "There is not a working man in Preston with whom I have not a personal acquaintance, and with whose habits I am not acquainted." He never, however, made any parade of what he did, and few will ever know, until the "great day" shall reveal it, the extent of his efforts, or the blessed results which he secured.

He believed in the religion of sunshine, and, as a consequence, he was ever on the alert to do anything which would help to promote the happiness of those who happened to be either poor or helpless. Among other things he originated a plan for letting a little brightness into their lives, by having cheap trips to the seaside. Every summer, the poorest of the town, "the halt, the lame, and the blind," the scavengers, the sweeps, and the workhouse people, were treated to a railway trip to Blackpool, Southport, Fleetwood, or some other seaside place. It began in 1845, and has continued, generally in the month of August, ever since. The names by which it is known are expressive: the "Poor People's Trip," the "Old Women's Trip," the "Butter-milk Trip." This last was so named, because for a number of years a truck load of butter-milk was taken for the use of the "trippers." At first 2,000 to 2,500 were taken, but it went on increasing until 4,000 were conveyed.

The two following quotations from his own autobiography will perhaps best illustrate his mode of looking at things, and the manner in which he felt they ought to be dealt with :—

"We want more *practical religion ;* more feeling, more sympathy for the suffering of others. We should seek out and save, if possible, those who appear to be lost. 'The want of sympathy,' said a late judge, 'is the sin of this age.' If *visiting* was made a Christian duty, not merely a duty of a committee, but the duty of all, according to their time and opportunities, we should then have a full acquaintance with each other, learning to bear one another's burdens, and thus fulfil the law of Christ. The influence of *caste* seems to be getting worse. A change is greatly needed. As much as possible we should all mix together, the rich

and the poor, the wise and the unwise, the good and
the wicked. Not that we need to renounce either
private property or private rights, but the mixing
should be one of kindness, humanity, love, charity, and
goodwill. What should we say of our street sweepers
if they were always sweeping in the clean places,
avoiding altogether the filth and dirt of the back
streets, accumulating and spreading their pestiferous
effects all around ? What should we say of our
medical men if infective diseases were allowed to get
so rife as to destroy thousands for want of their
attendance, their time being taken up with those who
least need them. I hold it equally important that
quite as great efforts should be made to remove *moral*
as physical evil.

"In all our Temperance labours we should get as
low down as possible. It is not the righteous, but
sinners, that need all our help. Christ condensed all
the commandments into *two,* one being this : 'Thou
shalt love thy neighbour as thyself.' But how can we
be said to love our neighbour whom we never see, never
call upon, and never inquire after ? Many teetotalers
are fond of 'demonstrations,' but those who take a
wider and more Christian view delight more in visiting and teaching the residents of the *slums,* helping
the downcast, remembering that we are all of one
flesh, children of the same parent. Here, indeed,
shines the bright example of the Lord Jesus. The
interests of the poor, the wicked, the lost, the friend-

less, were ever near His heart. He delighted in the companionship of the lowly. . . . If one in a hundred go astray, He teaches us that we should seek him out and bring him back, rejoicing more over his restoration than over the ninety-and-nine who remained in the fold. It is a question for temperance people to consider seriously how greatly behind they are in love, compassion, pity, kindness, and self-denial, their great Teacher, who went about doing good."

Ever on the lookout to do good, nothing calculated to accomplish seemed to escape his notice, or to be beneath his attention. On one occasion, while visiting among the poor, he found that coal was mostly sold to them by the bag, in which the dealer professed to put half, or a hundredweight. On weighing one of these bags, he found it was considerably short of the proper weight. With his usual practical sagacity he resolved to divide the town into districts, and fixing upon points near where the poor mostly lived, he sent cart-loads of coal, with scales for weighing it, which he sold at a little more than cost price, in this way giving the poor the full benefit, and at the same time he had the satisfaction of knowing that he drove the robbers completely out of the field.

Another illustration of the widespread character of his efforts may be mentioned. As a member of the Corporation and a Guardian of the Poor of Preston, he devoted a good deal of attention to the social welfare of the townspeople. He assisted in the removal of unhealthy dwellings, the straightening of streets, promoting open spaces, playgrounds, and parks, providing seats for the weak and weary, and opening of drinking fountains for men and beasts. All these things clearly illustrate how anxious he was to do all he could to promote the health, comfort, and beauty of the town of which he was a citizen.

During the American War, Mr. Livesey availed himself of another opportunity for showing his practical sympathy with the suffering poor. Owing to the stoppage in the supply of cotton in 1862, Preston, which was entirely dependent upon America for its supply of that material, suffered from the terrible Cotton Famine, which continued for nearly four years. Thousands of men, women, and children were out of work, although able and willing to do it. Some urged that relief should be given only through the Board of Guardians, but Mr. Livesey's warm heart hit upon a much more generous method. He used his influence to call a town's meeting. By his speech and subsequent hearty efforts, they succeeded in raising and distributing £131,000, and giving out to the famishing ones 5,141,418 tickets of relief.

Joseph Livesey was a practical reformer. If he saw an evil, he was not content with merely regretting its existence, and weeping over its victims, but he set to work in a business-like way to remedy it. Finding on one occasion, when he was visiting among the poor, that the sleeping arrangements of many of them were of the most wretched character, he at once set to work to improve them in this way. He persuaded the wives to empty the old bed-ticks and wash them, and he provided a supply of chaff to fill them ; where the ticks were too rotten to hold it, he assisted them to get fresh ones, and gave himself no rest till he knew they could sleep in comfort. Once he met with a poor sufferer lying on damp straw, covered with sores and ulcers. He went home, took his own feather bed, and, calling a cab, carried it, with the needful clothes to cover him, to the poor person. This kind of work so increased, that he appealed to others to help him, which led to the formation of.what was called " The Bedding Charity," by which thousands of clean beds for the needy and suffering have been provided.

Another striking incident in which the practical sagacity and shrewd common sense of Mr. Livesey showed itself was in connection with a serious disaster which overtook the people of Preston through the failure of the bank. In July, 1866, it stopped payment. As soon as the event became known, thousands of people were plunged into sorrow. The directors were paralysed, and hope fled. As soon as Mr. Livesey heard the sad news, he went at once to the bank, and asked for a full statement of their position. At once he grasped the facts, and saw a way out of the difficulty, which he laid before the directors. His courage and dogged determination inspired them with hope, and they consented to follow his advice. He then went out and addressed the despairing crowd, and told them, as they pressed round the door of the bank, what he was prepared to do. At once confidence was restored. Men who had given up all hope, and feared ruin stared them in the face, quickly lost their fears, and placed the fullest reliance upon the credit of his integrity and uprightness. The result was, that the bank was re-established, and he was, at the earnest solicitation of the shareholders, made a director.

Notwithstanding his busy life and active labours, yet he often lamented he had done so little. To one of his best friends and oldest fellow-worker, Mr. Thomas Walmsley, he said, a few months prior to his last moments on earth, "Thomas, what I regret the most is the little I have done in my life. Oh, do work as much as ever you possibly can." It was in this humble and modest manner that this truly noble and unselfish man viewed the vast labour and numerous efforts of his busy life. On another occasion, in reply to the expressions of wonder that he could find time to do so much, he wrote, "Whatever I engaged in I pursued with as much energy as if the success depended upon my exertions alone." Again, on the occasion of his eighty-fifth birthday, he said, in reply to a deputation from the Preston Society, that, "while he lived, and could handle a pen, while he had health, he would still consecrate his energy and influence in promoting the good old cause." How much better to speak thus than to have the sorrow of looking back upon either a useless, wasted, or wicked life.

Among the provisions found in Mr. Livesey's will, was one to the effect that a copy of his Malt Liquor Lecture should be presented to every householder in Preston. A special edition of 20,000 copies was prepared for the purpose, and the borough was divided into sixteen districts, each containing from 600 to 1,000 houses. A host of willing workers were supplied with a map, and a list of the streets to be visited. In this way the work was well and speedily done, and the people of Preston was once more reminded, on the 1st day of January, 1885, of Mr. Livesey's annual address on Temperance. Each copy was inscribed with the words, " He being dead yet speaketh."

With increasing years, his latter days were spent in peaceful retirement, now and then cheered by the thought that throughout a long and honourable career he had been engaged in spreading the principles of Temperance, and in this way scattering joy and gladness into many hearts and homes all over the world Gradually his sufferings increased, and on September 2nd, 1884, only a day after the fifty-second anniversary of the signing of that memorable pledge by the seven, he passed away peacefully to his rest, in the presence of his sons and other members of his family. As the *Daily News* truthfully said, "the usual commonplaces of regret were inapplicable, for he had died in the extreme fulness of years, and after his unselfish and humane labours had produced their beneficent fruits."

On the 5th day of September his remains were laid by the side of her who had been his true and faithful helpmate for fifty-four years. On the way to the resting-place hundreds might be seen, who had come from all parts of the country to testify their respect, while ten thousand people lined the streets with uncovered heads, as the solemn procession passed along, alike ready to own their appreciation of the noble work which had been done by the self-denying, persistent, and courageous pioneer of Temperance, JOSEPH LIVESEY.

PRINTED BV CASSELL & COMPANY, LIMITED, LA BELLE SAUVAGE, LONDON, E.C.